P9-CKW-195

Wendy

✡

KAREN WALLACE

SIMON & SCHUSTER BOOKS FOR YOUNG READERS
New York London Toronto Sydney

SIMON & SCHUSTER BOOKS FOR YOUNG READERS
An imprint of Simon & Schuster Children's Publishing Division
1230 Avenue of the Americas, New York, New York 10020

This book is a work of fiction. Any references to historical events, real people, or real locales are used fictitiously. Other names, characters, places, and incidents are products of the author's imagination, and any resemblance to actual events or locales or persons, living or dead, is entirely coincidental.

Originally published in Great Britain in 2003 by Simon & Schuster UK

The text for this book is set in Centaur MT.

Manufactured in the United States of America
10 9 8 7 6 5 4 3 2 1

CIP data for this book is available from the Library of Congress.
ISBN 0-689-86769-7

To Nick and Helena,

with love and thanks

Editor's Note

The spelling and punctuation throughout this work have been retained from the original British edition.

Wendy

1

'Your pa's fair posh,' said the butcher's boy to Wendy Darling when he saw her in the kitchen. He banged down a wide, flat box on the table. 'All the way from France, these are.' He looked sideways at Wendy's thick golden hair and her big, black-lashed blue eyes. *You'll break some hearts one day, young miss.*

'On your way, Eddie,' said Mrs Jenkins, the cook, firmly. 'And don't forget my sausages tomorrow. There'll be a cup of tea for you if they're fresh.'

Eddie grinned and left the kitchen. *That Mrs Jenkins, she had eyes in the back of her head.*

Mrs Jenkins turned to the box on the table. '*Baby* chickens!' she said in a disgusted voice. 'No taste to 'em at all! What's wrong with a good English cockerel straight from the farmyard?'

Wendy opened the box and saw twenty-four tiny feathered bodies lying side by side, packed in newspaper.

She picked one up. Its bones were fine as hairpins and its floppy neck was thinner than her finger. Mrs Jenkins was right. What was the point of them? Each bird seemed barely bigger than a mouthful. 'Can I help you pluck them, Mrs Jenkins?'

'If you put your apron on, dear.'

An hour later, Wendy watched as Mrs Jenkins seasoned the tiny chickens with thyme and wrapped them in fat bacon. 'There's not many knows how to keep 'em juicy,' she said to herself proudly, banging a body into the roasting pan. 'New-fangled nonsense!'

'Putrefaction,' said Wendy sternly.

'Yes, dear.' Mrs Jenkins was used to Wendy saying strange things. The girl was only nine but she often seemed more grown up than her age. She spent half her time with her head in a book and the other half grubbing about in the garden with her magnifying glass.

'It means rot.'

Wendy

Last summer, Wendy had wrapped a dead blackbird in greased muslin and buried it for a month, then dug it up and looked at it through the magnifying glass. Her brother John had been sick.

'It's what happens to dead things,' said Wendy to Mrs Jenkins. She drew her eyebrows together. 'Do you think these baby chickens have maggots inside? Extra wriggly *French* maggots?'

'I doubt your father would thank me for serving rotten meat.' Mrs Jenkins rolled her eyes. 'These birds cost a pretty penny, I can tell you.'

Wendy clicked her tongue. It would be just like her father to show off. He always had to have the latest thing. Then he had to make sure that everyone knew how clever he was.

'I think it's a terrible waste of money, Mrs Jenkins. Why can't Father's friends eat pigeon pie like we do? Then he could give the money he saved to the poor families who need it.'

By now all of the little birds were seasoned and wrapped in bacon. 'It's that Lady Cunningham,' said Mrs Jenkins in a flat voice. 'She and Sir Alfred are coming to the dinner this evening. Your father thinks she likes foreign food.' Mrs Jenkins picked up a chicken and jabbed the sharp end of a skewer in one end and out the other.

'Why are you stabbing them?' asked Wendy. She looked at Mrs Jenkins sideways. 'It's not their fault they're French.'

'I'm not stabbing them.' Mrs Jenkins laughed. 'It's the heat from the skewer that cooks them fast and keeps them juicy.'

'First they're strangled, then they're stabbed,' said Wendy. 'I'm glad I'm not French.'

'I expect your mother and father are too, dear.'

Mrs Jenkins slid the last two bodies onto their skewer and fitted them into the roasting pan. Wendy swung a wooden spoon back and forth in front of her face like a metronome. She stared at the huge Welsh dresser on the far side of the kitchen. Its shelves were stacked with china mixing bowls and metal moulds for jelly and baking tins for Mrs Jenkins's superb cakes. Underneath the shelves, copper-bottomed saucepans hung in a row according to size.

'Do you think the big preserving pan would sound like a drum and the tiny pot like a triangle if I hit them with this spoon?'

'I couldn't rightly say, dear,' said Mrs Jenkins, not really listening.

Wendy stared down at the row of wrapped bodies stuck with skewers.

'If God lets this happen to little birds, why shouldn't it happen to children? It says in the Bible –'

'Wendy!' snapped Mrs Jenkins. 'For goodness' sake, stop asking silly questions or I'll ruin these birds and your mother will have my guts for garters.'

'I'm sorry.'

Mrs Jenkins wished she hadn't spoken so sharply. She knew perfectly well that Wendy had hardly anyone to talk to besides her brother John, and even though he was seven, he seemed much younger. As for their nanny – well, Mrs Jenkins was convinced that women like Edwina Holborn should be dragged out at dawn and shot.

'Nothing to be sorry about,' said Mrs Jenkins in a kinder voice. 'But there's a time and place for everything.' She held out a white napkin folded into a parcel. 'Now, here's a treat for you. They're your mama's favourite and I made them specially.'

'Is it new-fangled foreign food?'

Mrs Jenkins smiled. 'Find out for yourself. Run along now, or that nanny will be after you.'

Wendy pulled open the napkin and saw a tiny glazed tart stuffed with a creamy filling. A sprinkling of black dots gleamed on the top. It looked more like a brooch than something you would eat. 'Thank you,' she said. But Mrs Jenkins had turned to a mountain of scallop shells in the shallow stone sink.

Two minutes later, Wendy was climbing up the back stairs towards the nursery. Everything was quiet, thank goodness. Horrible Nanny Holborn was still out with John and Michael at the Round Pond in Kensington Gardens.

Poor John and Michael.

She held the napkin parcel tightly in her hand. Mrs Jenkins was her favourite person in the house, after John and Nana, of course. As she reached the third flight of stairs, she heard Liza, the housemaid, singing from behind the ironing-room door, one of those music-hall songs about moonlight and violets. Wendy smiled to herself. Liza was really singing about Charlie Pickles, the carpenter's apprentice from the mews behind Kensington Place. It was supposed to be a secret but she had heard Liza telling Mrs Jenkins that she and Charlie were engaged to be married.

Wendy climbed up the last flight of stairs and turned down the corridor. It wasn't often Liza sang. Liza knew to keep quiet if Nanny Holborn was about. Nanny Holborn had lost two fiancés in the South African War so she didn't hold with men because all they did was let you down. If she ever heard Liza singing or saw her smiling to herself, Nanny Holborn always went into a fury. No matter how quickly Liza finished her work on her afternoon off, there was always an extra job waiting for her. More often than not it was well into the afternoon before Liza could pin on her hat and take a turn with Charlie around the park.

Poor Liza! She never used to have anything to do with Nanny Holborn. Then Agnes, the nursery maid, had given in her notice and her father hadn't taken on a replacement, which was odd because he always seemed proud that the Darlings had more servants than most of their friends. So Liza was doing two jobs now.

'Not that I mind too much,' she told Wendy. 'Me and Charlie'll need the money to get married. There just ain't enough hours in the day, that's all.'

Wendy crept quickly past the ironing-room door so as not to disturb Liza. She turned the brass handle of the nursery door as gently as she could and closed it softly behind her.

A big black Newfoundland dog looked up from a basket on the linoleum floor. She flopped her tail but didn't get up.

Wendy knelt down beside the basket.

'Nana,' she whispered, 'I've had an idea. It's probably really stupid.' She opened the white napkin parcel. 'Mrs Jenkins says this is one of Mother's favourite things.' She looked into the dog's brown, bloodshot eyes. It was her favourite thing to imagine that Nana could talk. 'I'm going to send myself into a trance like those snake charmers do in India. Then I'm going to eat this tart and see if I can imagine what it's like to be Mother.'

Nana looked at the tart, wrinkled her nose and rested her wide head on her paws again. *You're mad.*

Wendy buried her face in the dog's loose, glossy fur and laughed. 'Mother says that some mad people are really geniuses.' She held out the napkin in front of her and closed her eyes. Then she swayed from side to side and hummed tunelessly. A moment later she whisked the tart from the napkin and put the whole thing in her mouth.

It was absolutely disgusting.

What she had thought would be sweet creamy custard was a fishy mush that tasted sharp and rotten at the same time. The pastry was peppery and oily, and the shiny little black dots that should have been liquorice were salty and foul and popped in her mouth as if they were insects' eggs. Wendy spat the tart back into the napkin.

Heavy footsteps clumped up the stairs. Lighter footsteps pounded down the corridor.

'Wendy! Wendy!' shouted John at the top of his voice.

'Stop running!' snapped Nanny Holborn, 'or there will be no staying up this evening.'

The pounding stopped.

Wendy wiped her mouth on her sleeves. 'What am I going to do, Nana?'

I'll think of something.

'Hurry up!' croaked Wendy.

Wasting food was a sin close to blasphemy as far as Nanny Holborn was concerned. Every plate had to be cleaned. Every vile crust had to be properly chewed and swallowed. If not, it would appear without fail at the next meal.

Wendy looked down at the filthy mouthful of tart in the napkin. 'Nana! She'll make me eat it!'

'Wendy! Wendy! I can sail my boat by myself!'

John rushed into the nursery, holding up his sailboat like a trophy above his head. His brown eyes shone with excitement under his short, straight black hair. 'It worked, what you showed me!'

At the same moment, Nana pushed her nose into the white napkin parcel and gobbled up the tart in one mouthful.

John stared at his sister as she stuffed the napkin down the front of her pinafore. 'What –'

Wendy shook her head and put a finger to her lips.

'I didn't mean to,' Michael was wailing in the corridor. 'I couldn't help it. I promise, Nanny, I couldn't help it.'

Nanny Holborn appeared at the door, clutching Wendy's youngest brother by the collar. She was a tall woman with thin lips and a bony face and eyes that glinted like metal. She wore a long, navy-blue cloak and a high, black bonnet. Beside her, Michael howled and tried to pull away from her grip. He was dark-haired like his brother but his face was round and chubby.

'You're a nasty, dirty little boy,' snarled Nanny Holborn. She frogmarched Michael across the room towards a screen on the far side. 'And a disgrace to your family.'

'How does your boat sail, John?' asked Wendy quickly.

'Like a winner,' said John. 'She'll make a Channel crossing next.'

Nanny Holborn's head swung around like the muzzle of a gun. 'Did you lie down on your bed, as you were told?'

'Yes, Nanny,' said Wendy. She forced herself to look at Nanny Holborn's tin-coloured eyes. They were furious as usual. 'I looked at my encyclopaedias.'

'Did you let that filthy dog outside to do its business?'

'Yes, Nanny.' Wendy looked sideways at Nana.

Takes one to know one.

'Humph,' muttered Nanny Holborn as if she was trying to make up her mind about something. She disappeared behind the screen, dragging Michael with her as if he was a sack of dirty laundry.

'Please, Nanny!' cried John. 'You won't change your mind, will you?'

Wendy's heart thumped in her chest. Yesterday, Nanny Holborn had promised they could watch the guests go in to dinner and count the dishes of food that were carried in after them.

'I bet there will be more than a hundred plates, Nanny,' gabbled John hopelessly.

All they could see behind the screen was the back of Nanny Holborn's navy serge skirt and the tie of her white apron.

'We've been very good,' pleaded John. 'Haven't we, Wendy?'

'We have,' cried Wendy.

They heard a sticky wet sound as Nanny Holborn stripped off Michael's soaked trousers.

'I want to see Mother all shiny!' wailed Michael.

There was a hard slap, then a high-pitched scream.

Nanny Holborn appeared with Michael, half-naked, in her arms. A wide red welt was spreading across his upper thigh.

Michael buried his face in Nanny Holborn's hard starched collar and sobbed.

Metal screeched on linoleum as Nanny Holborn dragged a grey tin bath in front of the fire and tipped in two enormous jugs of hot water. Even though there was running water in the house, she insisted on bathing Michael like a baby. She tested the water with her elbow and plunged Michael into the bath. Then she turned to where Wendy and John were standing in the middle of the nursery.

'Don't stand there gawping,' she snapped. 'Eat your tea. Then bath and straight to bed for both of you.'

'But, Nanny!' cried John. 'You promised.'

Nanny Holborn fixed him with her crazy metal eyes. 'One more word out of you and you'll be sorry.'

'I hate her,' whispered John when tea was finally over and they had had their baths. 'I wish she was dead.' He stood on his tiptoes and hung up his wool dressing gown in the cupboard in their night nursery next door.

Wendy yanked off her own dressing gown and dropped it on the floor. 'Did you see the colour of Michael's leg?'

John bent down and picked up the dressing gown. The idea of any more trouble was unbearable.

'He's only four,' said Wendy furiously. 'Anyone can have an accident.' She pulled back her sheet and swung herself into the bed that was nearest the window. 'I'm going to tell Mother. I swear I will.'

John put his sheepskin slippers neatly together and climbed into his own bed. He lay down as still as a dead body. 'What good would that do?' he said. 'She couldn't look after us. Besides, she'd never believe you. Grown-ups never do.'

Wendy thought of the disgusting tart Mrs Jenkins had made for her mother. How could it be one of her favourite things? 'Grown-ups make me sick,' she muttered.

'Me too.'

Outside the window a hansom cab rattled to a stop on the cobbles. 'Number 14, guv,' said a voice. Money clinked. 'Very generous, guv.'

'The guests are arriving,' said John, sniffing.

There was a creak of bedsprings as Wendy slid out of bed and put on her dressing gown.

'Wendy,' whispered John in a horrified voice, 'what are you doing?'

She crept across the room and sat on her brother's bed. 'Nanny Holborn will be snoring by now,' she said in a low voice. 'Come on. She always falls asleep in front of the fire. I often sneak out to watch.'

John's eyes were wide in the dim light. 'Watch what?'

'Anything that moves or talks. I'm doing a survey of everything that happens in the house.' Wendy cocked her head. 'For example, so far I've discovered that Liza always examines her teeth in the landing mirror.'

'What if we get caught?'

'Don't be so wet! Do you want to see the guests arriving or not?'

'Of course I do,' said John sulkily.

'Then follow me and we won't get caught. I know a way across the nursery floor that doesn't creak.' Wendy fixed her brother with a stern eye. 'But you have to step exactly where I step. Do you understand?'

'OK. As long as you promise we won't get caught.'

'Trust me!' Wendy went over to the night-nursery

door and put her ear to the keyhole. 'Wait for my signal.' Then, more quietly than John could have believed possible, she turned the handle and opened the door.

The nursery was lit by the orange glow of the coal fire. In the corner, Michael was sound asleep in the nursery cot, curled up in a miserable hump with his thumb in his mouth. He had been put to bed on his own as a punishment for wetting his trousers. In front of the fire, Nanny Holborn was slumped in her padded wooden chair. Her white indoor cap had slipped down her forehead and a ball of wool had tumbled from her lap and lay beside a basket of socks on the floor.

Wendy held her breath and listened to the dragon's steady snores. Satisfied, she turned around and signalled to John.

2

Mrs Darling sat at her dressing table and stared at her reflection in the glass. Above her heart-shaped face and slightly tilted nose, the gold of her piled hair matched the gold-leaf pattern on her gauzy turquoise dress. A richly beaded bolero jacket in a darker turquoise showed off her tiny waist.

Mrs Darling was pleased with herself because she knew that she had chosen well. She looked beautiful and vulnerable, and certainly not old enough to have three children of her own.

Bradley, her lady's maid, looped another rope of pearls over her mistress's head. Her fingers still tingled from tugging at the silk cords that laced Mrs Darling into her whalebone corset. 'Will ma'am wear flowers tonight?'

Mrs Darling looked at the clusters of silk flowers she often wore in her hair in the evenings. None of them took her fancy. Suddenly her pleasure in her beauty disappeared and she felt a dull weariness creep over her. It wasn't that she didn't enjoy entertaining, just that she preferred less formal occasions. She liked seeing her friends on her At Home afternoons and having 'supper' rather than 'dinner', followed by bridge or a turn at the piano. It was her husband who liked to throw grand parties. He insisted that they helped his career. Mrs Darling knew the truth was that he wanted the opportunity to show off.

Bradley went over to the wardrobe and came back with a spray of blue-green feathers on a diamond clip. She fixed the jewel in Mrs Darling's hair. For a moment, neither woman spoke. They were both thinking the same thing.

'You have never looked so lovely, ma'am.'

Mrs Darling touched her maid's hand. 'Thank you, Bradley. You know I'd be lost without you.' She smiled. 'See that Cook gives you a second helping tonight.'

'Yes, ma'am.' Bradley bobbed and left the room.

Two floors below the front door bell rang.

Mrs Darling looked at her reflection for the last time. As she stared, her face seemed to disappear and only her eyes floated in the mirror in front of her. 'Gracious,' she murmured. She shook her head and got up from her dressing table. 'I'm going mad.'

A hansom cab rattled to a stop below. Mrs Darling opened her bedroom door and stepped gracefully down the stairs, her turquoise dress trailing behind her. As she followed the curved mahogany rail, two thoughts crossed her mind. She hoped that Mrs Jenkins would make a success of those ridiculous little birds. But even more strongly, she hoped that her husband wouldn't get drunk and behave like a hog.

Wendy led John to her usual place behind the banisters and they watched all the guests arrive. There were so many of them that even Wendy lost count. In fact, the only people she recognised were Sir Alfred and Lady Cunningham, and that was because they lived around the corner at Number 27. Their daughter Letitia was supposed to be Wendy's best friend, although how her parents could think such a thing was a mystery to Wendy. In the end, she decided that it didn't matter whether it was true or not. It was something they wanted to believe, so she let them. It was easier that way.

'What are they doing?' asked John.

All the guests had disappeared into the drawing room and there was no sign of food anywhere.

'They're drinking cocktails,' said Wendy. 'They're yucky mixtures of whisky and sugary sour stuff. Cowboys and grown-ups like them.'

'Ugh.'

Wendy shrugged. She thought again about Letitia, who had an eleven-year-old brother called Henry. Her father was going to send John to the same school as him. Wendy didn't like Henry. Once, he'd told her, he had roasted a live sparrow over a candle flame.

'Do you want to go to school with Henry Cunningham?' she asked.

John shook his head. 'He's always telling me about the horrible things that happen to new boys.'

'Ignore him,' said Wendy. 'He's a bully and a liar.'

At that moment, the guests moved like a gaggle of geese out of the drawing room and down the corridor into the dining room.

'One hundred and eighty-seven, Wendy!' whispered John. He waggled his fingers in front of her face. 'And eighty of them were puddings!'

Wendy nodded. It was good to see John happy. Most of the time Nanny Holborn went out of her way to tell him how stupid he was. She put her hand to her ear and listened out for the sound of snoring. The rumble was still slow and steady. This was good – any snorting or snuffling signalled danger. Down the stairs and behind the dining-room door there was a roar of voices, the clash of knives and forks on china and the tinkling of crystal glasses. John was delighted with the racket. But to Wendy the voices sounded like crows cawing in a field.

Suddenly Mr Darling's voice rose loud above the others. In her mind's eye, Wendy saw her father stand up from his place at the head of the table.

'To the women!' bellowed Mr Darling. 'Where would we be without 'em?'

'Hear! Hear!' There was a thunder of approval and a louder jingle of glasses.

At that moment the door opened and Liza appeared, carrying two half-eaten legs of roast lamb on a silver salver. Behind her a young Scots girl called Alice Jameson balanced three serving dishes of leftover vegetables on either arm. Alice often helped Mrs Jenkins in the kitchen. Tonight it had been decided that she was steady-handed enough to assist in the dining room.

'What a kerfuffle,' gasped Alice as she shifted the weight of the dishes on her arms. 'Are they always like that?'

'Master's drunk as a boiled owl,' said Liza, pushing open the door that led down to the kitchen. 'Mind yourself on these steps.'

From inside the dining room there was the sound of a glass smashing on the floor.

A clammy feeling crept over Wendy. A picture of her father's face floated inside her head – not his pink, smooth morning face as he left for the office, but his evening face, which she sometimes saw from her place behind the banisters when he came back from supper at his club or with Mrs Darling from a dinner party. Those times her father's face was always the same. His thick brown moustache was perfectly curled, but his straight nose and long cheeks were blotchy and the bones of his face looked soft, as if they were made of wax.

Suddenly Wendy wanted to go back to her bed as fast as possible. 'John – '

'I got it wrong,' said John, still counting his fingers. 'It was one hundred and ninety one.' He looked up at his sister. 'What did Liza say?'

'Something about lots of leftovers,' said Wendy. She was glad John hadn't heard. 'We must get back before Nanny wakes up.'

As they pulled themselves up on the stair rail, the dining-room door opened and Mr Darling and Lady Cunningham stepped into the hall.

Wendy watched as her father glanced quickly around him. His face looked sharp, like a fox's. She frowned. It was almost as if he was making sure no one was about. Then Wendy noticed that Lady Cunningham was leaning on her father's shoulder as if she was feeling faint. Except that she didn't look faint. Wendy frowned again. If she was ill or needed to go to the lavatory – *retire,* Lady Cunningham would say – then she should be with Mother, not alone in the corridor with Father.

Wendy began to feel frightened and she didn't know why. She turned to pull John away. But it was too late.

John was staring over the stair rail and the grin had gone from his face. Wendy looked at where her father was standing with Lady Cunningham.

Only they weren't standing any more.

Lady Cunningham was lying backwards over the hall table. Her black evening dress was cut low and edged with red satin roses. The swell of her bosom was clear in the light from the chandelier. Wendy watched Lady Cunningham's lips part and her dark eyes glitter over her hooked nose. Then she saw her father lean forward and kiss her on the mouth, as if he wanted to suck the life out of her body.

John stood rigid, like a rabbit caught in the light of a bright lamp. At the same moment, Wendy heard Nanny Holborn snort in her sleep and there was a *thump* as something fell on the floor. Wendy grabbed John's arm and dragged him up the stairs.

They padded quietly down the corridor and stopped dead in front of the nursery door. Wendy listened at the keyhole, then slowly and silently she turned the handle.

Nanny Holborn was still asleep.

Wendy signalled John to follow her. Then they crossed the creaky linoleum floor without making a sound and climbed into their beds.

'I can't sleep,' whispered John.

'Neither can I,' said Wendy.

After the relief of getting safely back to bed, all she could think about was what had happened in the hallway. Each time she remembered a little more. Now she saw her father's left hand reach under the satin roses of Lady Cunningham's black dress. She saw Lady Cunningham's fat white fingers slide down the lapels of her father's evening tail suit.

John sat up in bed. 'Maybe Lady Cunningham had a splinter in her mouth. Remember when the glass broke, Wendy? Maybe it was Lady Cunningham's glass. Maybe Father was trying to get the splinter out.'

Wendy was about to tell John not to be so silly, to ask how he thought a splinter could have got into Lady Cunningham's mouth in the first place. Then she saw the relief on his face and changed her mind.

'That's all it was, Wendy,' John said, and she knew that he had persuaded himself and was happy again. 'That's all it was.'

Next door, a chair creaked and a poker rattled

coals in the grate. There was a dull *clang* as Nanny Holborn hung the poker back on its stand.

'Pretend you're asleep if Nanny comes in,' she whispered more loudly than she meant to. 'No one must know what we saw. Promise me!'

John pulled a face. It seemed to him that Wendy was always pretending things were more important than they were. What was wrong with his father helping Lady Cunningham? It must be jolly nasty to have a splinter in your mouth. And considering how horrible Lady Cunningham was, it was jolly brave of Father to help her at all. It must have been like sucking venom out of a rattlesnake bite.

'John,' whispered Wendy again, 'promise me!'

So John said, 'Oh, all right.' Suddenly the door was flung open and Nanny Holborn was standing over them.

'What's *all right?*' she snarled.

Wendy's stomach turned over. The monster must have been listening at the door. But for how long?

'I – I –' stammered John.

Nanny Holborn bent down beside him. 'You got out of your beds, didn't you?'

'Yes, Nanny,' mumbled John miserably. 'But we didn't do anything!' He was beginning to get confused. 'I promise, Nanny. We didn't see –'

'You are bad, deceitful children,' snapped Nanny Holborn. She strode over to Wendy's bed and pinched her shoulder hard. 'And if I ever hear you ask your brother to keep secrets again, I'll take a cane to you.'

'I'm sorry, Nanny,' whispered Wendy. She clamped her teeth together so that she couldn't say any more.

'Not as sorry as you'll be tomorrow morning,' said Nanny Holborn in a dangerous voice. 'Sit up, both of you.'

John and Wendy watched as Nanny Holborn opened the doors to the medicine cupboard that was high on the wall. She reached inside and turned towards them with a spoon and a bottle of castor oil.

'Two spoonfuls each,' she snapped. 'That'll sort out your nasty thoughts good and proper.'

John burst into tears. The last time Nanny had made him swallow two spoonfuls of castor oil, he had felt sick for a whole day. Nanny Holborn tipped the bottle over a large spoon and wrenched John's head backwards. 'And none of your crocodile tears. You've only yourselves to blame.'

The oil glugged out onto the spoon.

'*Wicked* children,' said Nanny Holborn.

John cried himself to sleep but Wendy lay for hours staring at the ceiling, trying to ignore the evil taste in her mouth. She had rubbed her tongue and teeth with a corner of her sheet but it didn't make any difference.

Down on the street, she heard the heavy front door swing open. Then there were two sharp blasts on a pea whistle. That would be Gorman, the footman, summoning a hansom cab. At last the dinner guests were leaving. Again and again Wendy heard two whistle blasts followed by the clip-clopping of a horse's hooves over the cobbles, then the jingle of the horse's harness and the squeak of springs as the driver jumped down and opened the door.

If you please, madam. Steady as you go, sir.

A door slammed. The clip-clop of hooves faded into the night.

Finally everything fell silent.

It was only now Lady Cunningham wasn't in the house that Wendy let herself think, but every time she closed her eyes all she could see were Lady Cunningham's fingers sweeping across the black lapels of her father's evening suit.

Hot tears began to pour down her face. She tried to tell herself that it didn't matter. Her father was drunk. And he was stupid when he was drunk. It was one of the things she'd heard her mother say from her place behind the banisters. But then she remembered the way he had checked to make sure no one was watching. She remembered the glitter in Lady Cunningham's eyes and she knew for certain that what they had done they had done many times before.

Wendy clenched her fists under the bedsheets. Lady Cunningham was a hateful snob. All she wanted was lots of money and fashionable friends. How could her father love her more than her mother? Worse, how could she ever look her father in the face again? *I hate you, I hate you,* she screamed to herself. She felt as if her mind was splitting in two. How can you hate someone you love?

Wendy gnawed at her finger until it hurt. Maybe that was the problem. Maybe her father didn't love his family any more. Wendy knew he was often cross with her mother for not wanting to have lots of dinner parties. And he thought his daughter was too much of a tomboy. Once, when she had been sitting in her secret place behind the banisters, she had heard them arguing about her. 'She's a girl,' he had snapped. 'Why can't she be more ladylike? She should be out taking dancing lessons, not crawling about in the mud, putting beetles in boxes.' A horrible thought occurred to Wendy. *Letitia Cunningham takes dancing lessons. Maybe he likes her better than me.*

Light from the streetlamps passed through the gaps in the curtains and lay in stripes on the floor like the bars of a prison. All Wendy wanted to do was curl up with Nana so she could tell her what she had seen. Not that it would make any difference. But somehow telling someone, anyone, might make it easier to bear.

Wendy pulled her blankets around her shoulders. Nana was not someone. There was nobody she could talk to. Particularly not John. She must let John think what he liked and then he'd forget everything he'd seen.

As Wendy turned over, the secret settled around her neck like a lump of iron on a chain.

3

Letitia Cunningham half closed her heavily lidded eyes and practised a pout in front of the carved mahogany mirror that hung in the front hall. On either side of the mirror, two huge, bushy bamboo plants grew out of huge china pots. Among the spiky green leaves, Letitia had the look of a jungle animal. She had dark eyes and olive skin like her mother. Her black ringlets coiled like snakes over her shoulders and her clothes were like velvety tropical flowers. She was wearing her favourite black and yellow striped dress and had forced Nanny George to tie up her hair with scarlet ribbons. Nanny George always nagged her to wear the frilly white dresses and navy-blue pinafores that other girls of her age wore, but Letitia would have nothing to do with them, and her mother let her have her own way even if it meant going against Nanny George's orders. Because Lady Cunningham believed that drawing attention to yourself was the only way to move up in the world. She wanted Letitia to have a reputation for being clever and sophisticated, and if she looked unusual and exotic so much the better.

Half hidden behind the bamboo leaves, Letitia changed her pout into a smile, then a leer. Then she bared her teeth and growled out loud and imagined herself sinking her teeth in Nanny George's hand. That morning she had arranged to play Bloody Slaughter with her brother Henry, using all the cowboys and Indians in the toy box. Henry had made up the game and it was one of Letitia's favourites. There was lots of scalping and killing, which were the two main things Henry was interested in at the moment. Then everything had been ruined because Nanny George announced after breakfast that Lady Cunningham wanted Letitia to go and play with Wendy Darling. Normally Letitia would have kicked up a fuss and Nanny would have given in. But since it was her mother's idea she knew she couldn't get out of it.

Letitia didn't like Wendy Darling. She always made Letitia feel silly and shallow, and that made Letitia cross. The other thing that made Letitia cross was that Wendy had more toys than her and lots more dresses, but seemed too daft to notice. What Wendy liked doing best was reading and grubbing about in her garden. She had boxes and boxes of disgusting dead insects and she was always peering at them through her magnifying glass. 'Look at this bumblebee, Letitia,' she would say. 'See that spike? It's called a proboscis.' And Letitia would feel sick at the sound of the word, let alone looking at the thing. And if Wendy wasn't waving her magnifying glass around, then she was droning on about boring things like how animals in the Arctic had white fur so they could hide in the snow or how nobody knew why the dinosaurs had disappeared. Letitia didn't *care* why the dinosaurs had disappeared, or for white fur. Nobody wore it, so what was the point of having it in the first place? Wendy even liked going to the zoo, which was a complete waste of time as far as Letitia was concerned. In Letitia's view the only sensible outing was to Oxford Circus, because there were more shops in Oxford Street and Regent Street than anywhere else in the whole of London.

'Tough luck, sis,' Henry had said, painting more gobs of blood on his toy cowboys' faces. 'You think you've got problems! That wet smack John Darling has been foisted on me.' So Henry was doing his best to scare the wits out of the little tick. But it wasn't so bad for Henry. Letitia happened to know that he liked playing with John. It gave him a chance to bully someone else and make up for all the bullying he had to put up with at school. 'We'll get together later, sis.' Henry laughed meanly. 'Anyway, you'll have a spiffing time with Wendy.'

Letitia peered in the hall mirror again and thrashed her head around in the bamboos. She curled her fingers into claws and pretended she was scratching out Wendy Darling's eyes. Then she threw back her head and roared.

Esther Cunningham stood on the stairs. She was a tall, studious-looking young woman with the clear, level eyes she had inherited from her mother. She clutched a leather brief-case in her hand and fought back the urge to throw it at her half-sister's head. Really the child was little more than an animal. She had the same dark, greedy, glittery look as her loathsome mother and, if someone didn't take her in hand, she would grow up and become just like her. Esther would never understand why her father had married her stepmother. He loved books and music and discussion, just like Esther did. Lady Cunningham hardly ever set foot in the library, and the only discussion she indulged in was called gossip. A vague sadness washed over Esther. Even though her own mother had been dead for many years, she still missed her.

The bamboos crashed to the ground and Letitia

howled with laughter. She would blame it on the parlour maid. No one would ever know.

'Letitia! For goodness' sake, what are you doing?' cried Esther as she walked down the stairs.

Letitia smirked nastily. 'Mother says it's vulgar to carry briefcases.'

Esther ignored her and checked her reflection in the mirror. Under the curved brim of her close-fitting felt hat and tailored blue suit, her face was as neat as her clothes. Esther hated putting on a show. She liked things to be plain and efficient. Yet when she smiled, her face was anything but plain. It was the same smile her mother had once had – though the only person in the house who knew this was her father, because Esther rarely found anything to smile about when her stepmother and half-sister were anywhere near.

'Esther!' scowled Letitia, who hated being ignored. *'Mother says it's vulgar to carry briefcases.'*

'Your mother is entitled to her own opinions,' said Esther lightly. 'As it happens, a briefcase is exactly what I need to carry my books and papers.'

'Books and papers,' sneered Letitia. Her eye fell on a rolled-up newspaper in Esther's hand. She could see the letters SUF written across the top. 'That says SUFFRAGETTE, doesn't it?' she cried. 'You're going to one of your crazy women meetings, aren't you?' Letitia kicked the soil from the bamboo pots around the floor. 'Papa says suffragettes should be whipped and sent to the colonies.'

'I really don't know why you have to be so unpleasant all of the time. You know perfectly well my father would never say that.' Esther tried to change the subject. 'What are you doing today?'

'Mama says I have to play with Wendy Darling.'

'Lucky you,' said Esther. 'Wendy's a lovely girl.'

'She's stupid and boring.' Letitia scowled. 'I know *you* like her.'

'What nonsense,' said Esther. But it was true that she liked Wendy Darling. She reminded her of herself at that age – curious about everything yet often tempted to take things too seriously. They had spent many afternoons together in the park, with Wendy talking about everything from how tadpoles could breathe under water to how God could have made the world in six days. Wendy didn't believe it was possible. Even if he did rest on a Sunday. Nor did Esther. Esther sighed. How different things would be if she had a half-sister like Wendy. 'Well, I hope you won't be unkind to her.'

'I'll be what I like.'

'Yes, I'm sure you will.'

This wasn't how Letitia wanted things to go at all. She wanted a fight. That was always more fun. Sometimes she even managed to make Esther cry, which was the best fun of all.

'At least I'm not a menace to society,' Letitia said sweetly.

Esther's patience ran out. 'If I have any more rudeness from you, Letitia, I shall tell my father I found you prying in my desk again. And this time, I shall make sure you get punished.' She rang the servants' bell.

'Yes, Miss Esther.' Nellie, the parlour maid, appeared in the drawing-room doorway. From the look on her face, Esther knew she had heard everything.

'Take Letitia back to the nursery,' said Esther. 'She is not to be trusted downstairs on her own.'

'You can't tell me what to do.' Letitia's mouth twisted into a snarl. 'Only Mother can.'

'Your mother will not be out of bed till eleven,' replied Esther coolly. 'Ask her then, if you like.'

'I hate you,' screamed Letitia. She turned and ran up the stairs.

Esther rubbed her hand over her face. 'Oh dear,' she sighed.

Nellie had been a parlour maid when Esther's

mother was alive. She was only working in the house now because Sir Alfred had insisted she stay. If Lady Cunningham had had her way, Nellie would have been sent packing, along with the other servants and most of the carpets and curtains and furniture she had inherited.

'She's nothing but trouble, that one,' muttered Nellie.

Esther nodded and pulled open the front door. 'I feel sorry for Wendy Darling.'

'Jump up, children,' cried Mrs Darling in her silvery voice. She sat cross-legged in her oyster satin bedjacket and patted the coverlet as if John and Wendy were pet dogs.

'Henry Cunningham has asked John to his house and Letitia is to come here to play with Wendy. Isn't that exciting?' Mrs Darling held out two tiny pieces of bread and honey. 'Lady Cunningham asked especially during dinner last night.'

Wendy stared hard at her mother's face for signs that she knew what had happened last night. There were none. Mrs Darling's skin glowed and her eyes shone. If anything she looked more beautiful than ever. *Unless she was hiding it.*

'I don't like Henry, Mother,' said John, not looking up. 'He twists my arm and anyway my tummy hurts today.'

'Don't be silly, dear,' said Mrs Darling, popping the bread and honey into her own mouth. 'Henry's a sweet boy.'

'Henry's a bully, Mother,' said Wendy stoutly. 'And I would much rather not play with Letitia today.'

'Goodness me, what a crosspatch! Why ever not?'

'I've got an infection.'

Usually the word 'infection' worked wonders with her mother. Mrs Darling was terrified of her children catching a disease, mostly because they might pass it on to her.

'Nonsense!' cried Mrs Darling. 'Letitia loves to play with your dolls' house and Lady Cunningham says the poor little girl doesn't have one of her own at the moment.'

'That's because she smashed it.'

'Wendy! What's got into you!' exclaimed her mother. 'You know perfectly well the nursery maid knocked it over and it's taking for ever at the mender's.'

Wendy nodded glumly but didn't speak. Letitia had already told her herself that the reason she had kicked in her own doll's house was that it was smaller than Esther's old one, which Esther wouldn't let her anywhere near. So to get her revenge she had searched Esther's writing desk for letters she could show her mother. But she didn't find anything interesting. *Just a lot of boring suffragette stuff.* It didn't occur to Letitia that Wendy might not think exactly like she did. The truth was that Wendy would have loved to have had a sister like Esther. It was Esther who had told her she wasn't peculiar for reading encyclopaedias and it was Esther who said that reading and going to proper school were the only ways a woman could learn to think for herself.

'So,' said Mrs Darling brightly, 'that's settled, then.'

No, it's not, said Wendy to herself. *Nothing's settled. Nothing's settled at all.* But she kissed her mother on the cheek because that was the easiest thing to do. And right now that was the best she could manage.

Half an hour later Wendy sat in front of her doll's house and sighed. It was set up for playing Rosegrove. Even John liked playing that game, because Rosegrove was Uncle Arthur's house in the country and it was where Wendy and John and Michael spent most of their summers. At Rosegrove there were woods and streams and stables with ponies. There was John's great friend Peggy, who was the carpenter's daughter, and Wendy's special friend Thomas, who was Peggy's brother. Thomas was special because everyone except Wendy said he was soft in the head. He didn't do anything all day but paint. But Wendy was sure Thomas was a genius and that she had been chosen to help him. So when John went off to build dens with Peggy, Wendy went down to the carpenter's cottage and read to Thomas, and whatever she read he painted. There was something magical about being with Thomas and Wendy didn't really understand it. All she knew was that she was happier with him than with anyone else in the world.

Now she packed up the cardboard trees John had made for the woods and put the wagonette back in its stable beside the brown horse called Brandy. They even had a doll they called Peggy, although John would die of shame if Peggy ever found out. Last of all she picked up her Thomas doll, which was much bigger than Peggy because Thomas was almost fifteen. She held him in her fingers and kissed his forehead. 'Dear Thomas,' she whispered. 'How can people think you're crazy? They should spend a week with Nanny Holborn.' And she put Thomas and Peggy in the carpenter's cottage she kept in the toy cupboard. There was no way she was going to play Rosegrove with Letitia. Letitia would sneer and say something horrible. 'Then I'd brain her with the poker,' she said to Nana, who was watching from her basket. 'And they'd send me to jail.'

Nana flopped her tail. *Bad idea.*

'I'll have to think of something she'd like,' said Wendy aloud. Because she knew from experience that if Letitia was happy, she was usually nice. So Wendy put out John's collection of cars and omnibuses and thought up a game called Lords and Ladies Spend the Weekend at a Large House in the Country. She even found a footman in livery and put him outside the front door. 'That'll keep her happy.'

Nana yawned. *Rather you than me.* She rested her head on her paws and went to sleep.

* * *

An hour later Wendy was sitting beside Letitia, wishing with all her heart she was somewhere far away. Even Mars would be too near. From the moment Letitia had arrived, she had thrown herself into Wendy's new game with gusto and insisted on playing out every domestic detail with a precision that was making Wendy feel more and more uncomfortable.

'Give me that bathtub,' demanded Letitia, picking up the stub of a pencil.

'Why?'

'Because Lord Caynham's man has to clean it before his lordship can bathe,' replied Letitia in a matter-of-fact voice.

'But it's not dirty.'

'Of course it is,' replied Letitia. She grabbed the porcelain tub and began to scribble around the inside edge. 'Lord Kington has shaved in it.'

'That's disgusting!'

'Maybe it is, but all lords shave in their baths. Everyone knows that.'

Letitia patted Wendy's arm. 'Is breakfast ready?'

'Almost.' Wendy gathered up a pile of cardboard cutouts she had coloured.

'Hurry up,' snapped Letitia.

Earlier Letitia had given instructions for hams, tongues, galantines and cold game birds to be laid out on one sideboard in the dining room. On another sideboard Wendy had had to make a row of spirit lamps to warm the oval dishes of kidneys, bacon, sausages and a steaming mound of kedgeree. Then she had had to colour in extra porridge because Letitia said there wasn't enough.

'Where's the ptarmigan?' demanded Letitia. 'Lord Kington must have cold ptarmigan for breakfast.'

'Why do they have to eat so many birds?' muttered Wendy, reaching for the scissors.

'Because they like them,' replied Letitia firmly.

Letitia guided the dolls' house through an astonishingly busy day. The lords and ladies and all their friends progressed smoothly from breakfast to the library, followed by a tour of the garden. Then it was time to change for lunch. After lunch they separated into little parties. Some walked in the rain. Others played bridge. In no time at all, it was tea and another change of clothes. Afterwards they sat and gossiped. At last their hostess, Lady Kitty Kington, who was very keen on cards, rose from the bridge table and went to dress for dinner. By now Letitia was jumpy and pink in the face. It was as if she had a big surprise she was trying hard to keep secret. She said, 'Have you laid out Lady Kitty's evening dress, Roberts?'

Wendy frowned. 'Why are you calling me Roberts?' A minute ago she had been Lady Eleanor Saville, recently presented to Queen Alexandra and rumoured to be engaged to a Captain Williams of the Welsh Guards.

'You're Lady Kitty's maid. Her last maid was called

Roberts, so you're called Roberts. Now, which dress have you laid out?'

If Wendy hadn't decided to do everything she could to make Letitia happy, she would have stopped the game right then and there.

'Cat got your tongue, Roberts?' snapped Letitia.

'Lady Kitty will wear the turquoise silk with the beaded jacket,' said Wendy, then realised it was the one her mother had worn the night before.

'An excellent choice, Roberts.'

'And what is Lady Caynham wearing?'

'The green tulle edged with lace,' replied Letitia in an edgy voice. 'And her belt with the emerald buckle.'

A few minutes later Letitia sounded the dinner gong and the house guests sat down at the table.

'The first course is spring soup, followed by salmon with caper sauce and oyster patties,' said Letitia. 'Lady Kitty will not steer the conversation as she did at luncheon, she will leave her guests to their own devices.'

Wendy sighed with relief. At last it seemed that this horrible game was almost over.

'Are the bedrooms prepared?'

Wendy nodded. Every grate glowed with a fire of crunched-up orange tissue paper and there was a tiny bottle of mineral water on each bedside table.

'Has the kitchen maid left a plate of sandwiches in every bedroom?' demanded Letitia.

Wendy nodded again.

'Are they covered with a linen napkin?'

'Yes.'

'Excellent, Roberts.' A smile flickered across Letitia's face. 'I'd say it's almost time for our guests to retire for the night.'

As she spoke she leaned forward and picked up the doll that was Lady Caynham and the doll that was Lord Kington.

'Goodness gracious,' cried Letitia. 'What on earth is happening here?'

Letitia rubbed the dolls' faces together and bent them backwards over a chair in the hallway.

'No, no!' cried Wendy.

'Yes,' shouted Letitia.

Wendy watched in horrible slow motion as Letitia marched the dolls up to a bedroom, pulled back the tiny swan's-down coverlet and laid them on top of each other across the double bed.

She turned to Wendy with a triumphant smirk. 'Lady Caynham and Lord Kington will be happier here, don't you think?'

Wendy had no idea what she was talking about. A horrible taste of bile rose in her throat. Her hands flew to her mouth. ' I – I –'

'Oh, don't worry about Lady Kitty,' said Letitia knowingly. 'Of course she's the hostess, but as long as no one finds out, she doesn't care what Lord Kington does.'

Wendy was sick all over the nursery floor.

* * *

John twisted his wrists inside their ropes and wondered why Henry Cunningham had to tie him so tightly to the nursery chair. Maybe it was because he had lost so badly at Bloody Slaughter. But what else could he have done? Henry's cowboys shot his Indians before they even had time to grab their tomahawks. Then, to make things worse, the cowboys had scalped the Indians they had just killed, which left John looking completely hopeless.

'There's nothing like a red-hot ramrod for making tongues wag,' snarled Henry Cunningham, waving the metal tip of an umbrella a few inches from John's face. 'Placed near the eyes, it's a wonderful persuader.'

'I say, Henry,' cried John, trying to turn his head away.

A nasty smile spread across Henry's jowly face. He held the tip of the umbrella against John's cheek. 'When it insinuates its way into the flesh, it can make the dumb speak.'

'I say, Henry,' cried John again. He could not stop his voice going squeaky and frightened. 'This isn't the thing at all. I mean, you told me you wanted to practise your knots.'

'Are you calling me a liar?' shouted Henry. He jerked the piece of rope that bound John's wrists together. 'What do you call that?' He jerked harder. 'Well?'

'A knot,' croaked John.

'Quite so,' said Henry. He strode across the nursery to where a coal fire burned in a grate behind a high brass fender and pulled out a smoking poker. 'Nicholls took the red-hot ramrod and whirled it twice in the air,' he shouted.

'Henry!' cried John, trying not to sound as if he was pleading. 'For goodness' sake!'

'Goodness?' hissed Henry. 'What's goodness got to do with it?' He began to creep forward with the poker in his hand.

John shouted with terror, pushing back with his

feet. The chair tipped sideways and hit Henry on the leg.

'Bugger!' yelped Henry, and dropped the poker on the carpet. A stink of burning wool filled the room. 'Now look what you've done!' He snatched up the poker and put it back in the grate.

'It was you, not me,' spluttered John.

Henry Cunningham narrowed his eyes to vicious slits. 'Haven't I told you what happens to sneaks at our school?'

John swallowed hard. Just the mention of Henry's school was enough to make his insides turn watery.

'Now, then. Who dropped the poker?' asked Henry, squeezing John's earlobe between his finger and his thumb. 'Who burned the carpet?'

'I did,' croaked John. 'Is that what you want?'

'Capital,' cried Henry. 'That'll do nicely!' He untied John's ropes and danced around him like a triumphant goblin. 'You're getting the hang of it!' Then, as if nothing had happened, Henry helped John up from his chair and put his arm around his shoulder.

'Have you ever seen a peepshow?' he whispered wetly in John's ear.

John shook his head. 'What's a peepshow?'

'It's like you peep through a keyhole and see, uh, things.'

'What things?'

Henry led John over to the other side of the nursery, although they both knew no one could hear them. 'Things you'd never believe, old boy.' His face lit up with glee. 'I've got some postcards. They're *really disgusting!*'

'It must have been something you ate,' said Liza, plumping up the pillows on Wendy's bed. 'I'll tell Nanny when she comes in.'

Wendy stood by the side of her bed, waiting to get in. 'Please don't tell Nanny.'

'Why ever not?'

'Because she'll give me castor oil again. I know she will.'

'Castor oil?' cried Liza. 'Why on earth would she do that?'

'It's her way of punishing us.'

'But you haven't done anything wrong.'

'She gets cross with us if we are ill.'

'Dear God,' muttered Liza. She pulled back the covers and tucked Wendy in.

Liza had heated the bed with a hot-water bottle, but Wendy couldn't stop shivering. 'Where's Letitia?'

'Alice took her home. But she asked me to tell you what a lovely time she had.'

Wendy turned her face to the wall so that Liza wouldn't see the tears running down her cheeks. 'I want Nana,' she whispered. 'Please, Liza. I'll send her away when I hear Nanny coming.'

Liza didn't know what to do. She knew as well as

Wendy that Nanny Holborn thought Nana was a dirty brute that shouldn't be allowed in the house. If she ever found out that Nana had been in the night nursery, she'd go berserk. But Liza had never seen Wendy so miserable and she was sure it was something to do with Letitia. In Liza's opinion, Letitia was a proper little madam and deserved a good hiding. But there was more to it than that. At breakfast, that monster Nanny Holborn had poured water into their porridge, with no cream or brown sugar. And the children had looked terrible, white-faced and red-eyed, as if they'd been awake half the night. She was a proper horror, that woman. God only knew what else she did to them. Whenever Liza undressed Wendy, she always looked out for any marks or bruises. Not that she would have known what to do if she found any. Tell Mrs Jenkins, probably.

Liza sat down on Wendy's bed and smoothed her damp hair away from her forehead. 'All right,' she said. 'I'll let Nana come in, but don't tell Nanny or I'll get the sack. Promise?'

'I promise,' whispered Wendy.

Nana stood by the bed and pushed her nose into Wendy's hand.

Wendy sat up and buried her face in the dog's neck. 'Nana,' she whispered, 'Is it true what Letitia said? Is it true Mother wouldn't care what Father does as long as no one finds out?'

Who knows what grown-ups think? You'll never understand.

'George Darling is a stockbroker. He depends on luck,' said Sir Alfred Cunningham. 'It's not a state of affairs of which I approve.'

'How is it a question of luck?' replied Lady Cunningham, looking up from the letter she was writing. 'Our children play together. I really cannot understand what you have against them.'

'Stocks and shares are unreliable,' replied Sir Alfred. 'And I believe George Darling is unreliable too. Jolly good baby chickens, though,' he murmured to himself. 'Ludicrous, of course.'

'Alfred,' cried Lady Cunningham crossly, 'I am not here to discuss food. In simple civility, we must ask them back.'

Sir Alfred Cunningham put down his newspaper. 'Victoria, you don't appear to be listening to me. I will put it simply. I don't approve of George Darling and I don't trust him. His wife is another matter. My uncle shot with her father at Rosegrove. Her brother is a perfectly decent man. And of course I don't mind Henry and Letitia playing with their children. But I don't want to get mixed up with them.'

Victoria Cunningham picked at the blotter on her writing table. Twelve years before, Alfred Cunningham had been exactly the match her factory-owning family had wanted for their daughter – a quiet widower with a title, plenty of money and a large house in fashionable Kensington. Victoria hadn't minded then that he was a little awkward in the sort of society she felt he should have been used to. His title made it easier to ignore the fact that he was a full head shorter than her and obviously preferred the company of his nine-year-old daughter, Esther, to that of other adults. Victoria had planned her campaign carefully. She had joined his Amateur Lepidopterists' Society and put up with the boring butterfly nets and stinking killing-bottles, not that she cared whether the butterflies lived or died. Although even worse than faking an interest in natural history had been faking an interest in plain, serious Esther. But the stakes had been high and Victoria had played her cards well. The moment Sir Alfred had laid his flushed face on her bosom, she knew he was trapped as surely as one of his own butterflies.

Sir Alfred shook out his newspaper. 'Is that all you wanted to talk about?'

Lady Cunningham looked up into her husband's fine-boned face. During their courtship, she had been so busy with her own plans that she had not noticed that his bumbling manners hid an iron will and a fierce intelligence. Furthermore, his views on fidelity were distinctly old-fashioned and not at all like those of the fast set Lady Cunningham was so keen to join. She had had to be very careful to hide her tracks where George Darling was concerned. It would be stupid to ruin everything now.

'I'm worried about Esther,' she said, holding her husband's eyes with a careful softening of her own. 'Really, Alfred, the women she sees! Some of them are held together with safety pins.'

'I take it you are referring to her suffragette friends.'

'Esther will never be accepted in society if she continues with this madness.'

'Esther will go her own way, Victoria. Frankly, I don't think she is much interested in the kind of society you are talking about.' Sir Alfred stood up. 'She comes into her inheritance on her next birthday and then she will be off our hands.' He touched his wife's cheek. 'You mustn't worry about her. She's a sensible young woman.'

'I don't call waving banners and shouting at policemen sensible,' snapped Lady Cunningham, pulling a face. 'Lady Mansfield said at Mrs Hamilton's At Home last

Tuesday that suffragettes should be birched and deported like convicts. I must say I agree with her.'

'Well, I don't. It seems perfectly reasonable to me that women should be entitled to vote. It is a fundamental right.'

'In that case they should moderate their language.' Lady Cunningham stabbed her blotter with her pen. 'Yesterday Nanny George found Letitia in tears after reading one of Esther's dreadful pamphlets.'

Sir Alfred sighed. Two weeks ago Esther had complained to him that she had caught Letitia rifling through her desk. 'She spies on me, Father,' Esther had said furiously. 'And her mother encourages her.' Nonsense, he had said. Now he wasn't so sure.

'Esther keeps her private papers in her desk,' said Sir Alfred evenly. 'Letitia must have found her pamphlets there.'

'That's ridiculous. Letitia would never do such a thing.'

'That's not what Esther thinks.'

Lady Cunningham tossed her head angrily. 'So Letitia is spying on her, I suppose?'

Sir Alfred felt a weary certainty that it was time to change the subject. 'No, no,' he said, and found himself looking at his wife's earrings. They were two pearls the size of damsons, fixed in yellow gold and surrounded with rubies. Sir Alfred did not like them. He never usually commented on his wife's taste, but these earrings looked like fairground baubles. They did not go at all well with the brooch at her collar, a plain amethyst that had belonged to his grandmother. He cupped a shiny earring in his hand. 'New?'

'My mother's,' said Lady Cunningham quickly. 'Don't you like them?'

'A trifle showy perhaps. I'm sorry,' he said, seeing the blood rise in his wife's neck. 'I've offended you.'

Lady Cunningham stood up. 'I shall change them immediately.' And she walked out of the room.

Two minutes later, she sat in front of her mirror, her eyes huge with rage. From a photograph on her dressing room wall, her husband stared at her with his infuriating all-seeing gaze. 'Interfering old fuddy-duddy,' a voice screamed in her head. 'I'm sick to death of your airs and graces.' She unhooked the earrings George Darling had given her the week before and put them away at the back of her drawer.

'So why were you sick yesterday?' asked John.

He and Wendy were walking as far as they dared behind Nanny Holborn and Michael through the park towards the Round Pond. Their excuse was that Wendy wanted to roll her hoop on the path and did not want it hitting anyone and getting them muddy.

'Who told you I was sick?' said Wendy sharply.

'I heard Liza tell Alice. Don't be cross. I was just wondering, that's all.'

Wendy whacked her hoop with her stick. There was no point in telling John the truth. He wouldn't understand and it would just upset him. Not that she understood much more herself. When she thought about it now, she didn't feel sick, only furious.

'I *hate* Letitia!' said Wendy. 'She's a liar and she's disgusting.'

John stared at his sister's angry white face. 'What do you mean, she's disgusting?' He looked down at his sailing boat. 'Henry showed me some postcards yesterday. He said they were disgusting.'

Two dolls rubbing against each other flashed into Wendy's mind. 'What was on them?'

'That was the strange bit.' John shrugged. 'It was just a man pushing a woman onto a bed. What's disgusting about that?'

'Nothing,' said Wendy quickly. She didn't want to say anything that might remind John of what he had seen from the banisters and make him question his splinter theory.

'Did he show them to Letitia?' she asked as casually as she could.

John nodded. 'But she said she already knew about that sort of thing. So Henry called her a liar, then she tried to rip up the postcards. They're really nasty, those two.'

Wendy hit her hoop so hard it fell over.

'Can I have a go?' asked John suddenly.

'If you want.'

'Hold my boat, then.' He ran off down the path, bowling the hoop in front of him.

Wendy stared at the boat in her hands. Her eyes filled with tears and it went all blurry. Now that John had told her about the postcards, maybe he felt better, but it just made her feel more lonely. All over the park families were sitting in groups, talking and laughing in the warm

Saturday sunshine. It seemed to Wendy that no one in her family had laughed for ages. Perhaps London was part of the reason. Everyone was always in such a rush in London.

Rosegrove was different. No one was in a hurry there. And everything was bright and colourful, not grey and greasy like London. You couldn't even ride on the top of an omnibus without getting covered in dirt. Wendy pretended she wasn't in the park at all. She was walking down the path to the vegetable garden at Rosegrove. It was a lovely place, with neatly clipped box hedges and rows and rows of flowers specially grown for the house. The boat in her hand was a basket. She was picking peas and beans to take to Mrs Crocker. That was how she'd met Thomas. Mrs Crocker sewed all the linen for her Aunt Emily at Rosegrove and she also made clothes for Mrs Darling. One afternoon Wendy had filled a basket full of vegetables and gone with her mother, who was having a fitting. Most people avoided Thomas. Often he howled and rocked if there were strangers in the house, but when he saw Wendy, it was as if he'd been waiting for her. His face lit up and he grabbed her in his arms.

Wendy began to run through the park.

'Oi! Watch where you're going!' A little boy in a sailor suit kicked a ball across her path. 'Are you stupid or something?'

Wendy stared down at the ball by her feet. She took one look at the little boy's weaselly face and kicked it as hard as she could across the grass.

'Serve him right,' said a voice behind her. Alice Jameson was carrying a big picnic basket. 'You were running like a hare, I could hardly keep up with you.'

Wendy stared at Alice's round face. 'Are you going on a picnic?'

'Me?' Alice laughed. 'Hardly! Mrs Jenkins keeps me far too busy for that.' She hefted the picnic basket strap onto her other shoulder. 'Didn't Nanny Holborn tell you?'

'Tell me what?'

Alice couldn't believe her ears. Wendy obviously had no idea what she was talking about. Liza was right. The woman was a monster.

'You are having a lovely family picnic,' said Alice as gaily as she could. 'Your mother ordered it specially from Mrs Jenkins.'

'Will Father be there?' asked Wendy, holding her breath. 'He usually goes out in his motor car on Saturdays.'

'Then he must have changed his mind,' said Alice. 'Or perhaps your mother changed it for him.' She pointed across the grass. 'There they are.' Wendy saw her parents immediately. Her father sat stiffly on a folding wooden chair, watching as Liza knelt on the edge of a tartan rug and set out plates and glasses. Even from far away, Wendy could tell by the hunch of his shoulders that he was cross. Her mother lay propped up on one elbow on the rug at his feet. Mr Darling didn't approve of lying on rugs – they left fluff on his trousers. A few yards away, Nanny Holborn sat on a stool with her back to a chestnut tree and watched Michael, who was chasing pigeons.

Usually Wendy loved picnics, and part of her wanted to run across the grass and hold out her hand for a huge tumbler of Mrs Jenkins's home-made lemonade. If only her father hadn't done what he'd done. Or maybe if only she hadn't seen him. *What you don't know can't hurt you.* Nanny Holborn had said it a million times. But Wendy knew it wasn't true.

'I can't believe your nanny didn't tell you.' Alice clicked her tongue impatiently. 'Mrs Jenkins said this was the first picnic she had made for you this summer.'

'Nanny Holborn doesn't like picnics,' said Wendy.

'That's no reason to ruin it for other people,' said Alice before she could stop herself.

Wendy looked into Alice's round, flushed face. 'Don't be cross with her, Alice. It will make her think she's won.'

Good Lord, thought Alice, as she shifted the heavy basket back onto her other shoulder. *Liza's right. There is something wrong going on in that nursery.*

'Isn't this divine?' Mrs Darling pulled down her hat to shade her face. A line of shiny pearl buttons on her grey and white blouse twinkled in the sun. 'So much more fun than driving about in a dirty, dusty motor car! Don't you think, George?' she added in a teasing voice.

George Darling wiped his mouth with a linen handkerchief for the second time. He had a horror of food sticking to his moustache. It made one look so ridiculous. 'You know perfectly well I do *not,*' he replied testily.

Across the park, he could hear the roar and splutter of motor cars churning along Kensington Gore to Knightsbridge. It was one of his favourite sounds. He could never understand why his wife disliked motor cars so much. It wasn't as if the clothes one wore were unattractive.

For her last birthday, he had given her a splendid hooded cloak made of mustard-yellow wool and edged with burgundy to match his yellow Lanchester with the red leather seats. She hadn't worn it once. At the thought of it, Mr Darling became so irritated with his wife that he moved his chair away from her and put it down beside his daughter.

'Come along, Wendy! Nothing worse than a hole in the conversation. What do *you* think of motor cars?'

Wendy looked up from the daisy chain she was making. 'I'm afraid I don't like them,' she said. 'I think they are smelly and they hurt horses.'

'Well said, sugar mouse!' cried Mrs Darling, laughing.

George Darling glared at his wife. 'Who cares about horses?' he snapped. 'Their day is over. Mark my words, young lady, in a few years there won't be a single horse left on the streets.'

Wendy shifted sideways to get away from the smell of her father's tobacco and hair oil.

'For heaven's sake, child! What's wrong with you? Anyone would think I'm a monster.'

Mrs Darling sat up. 'What nonsense you talk, George.'

'It's not nonsense,' said Mr Darling in a voice suddenly much too loud. 'She's been creeping about the house for two weeks now. And every time she sees me, she runs away.'

'You don't understand, Father,' said John, as if he was trying to explain something very complicated. 'Wendy's doing a survey of everything that happens in the house. That's why you think she's creeping about.' He looked proudly at his sister. 'She's not. I expect she's taking notes.'

'Shut up,' hissed Wendy.

John looked at her as if she had slapped him in the face.

'I've never heard such nonsense,' muttered Mr Darling. To Wendy's relief, he then turned back to his wife. 'I don't see why I should waste precious Saturdays with such idiotic children. I'd rather be motoring.'

'I care for you, Papa,' shouted Michael. He scrambled across the rug and put his hands on Mr Darling's arm.

Mr Darling shrank from Michael's sticky fingers. He picked up a piece of shortbread and began furiously crumbling it all over the rug.

'Good idea!' cried Michael, grabbing the pile of crumbs. 'Let's feed the ducks!'

'Let's feed the ducks *all together!*' cried Mrs Darling. She stood up and put her hand anxiously on her husband's shoulder. 'After all, it's not often we have a family picnic, is it?'

Nobody moved.

Mr Darling wiped his moustache again and stared

sulkily at the pile of crumbs. Wendy watched her mother fiddle unhappily with the pearl buttons on her blouse. Letitia's theory was wrong. Now she was positive her mother had no idea what was going on with Lady Cunningham. If she had, she wouldn't be putting up with her father's babyish behaviour. Really, Father was disgusting. She hated him.

'I can sail my boat!' shouted John desperately. Everything was ruined and he didn't know why.

Mr Darling stood up and dusted imaginary crumbs off his trousers. 'Splendid idea!' He took the boat from John's hands. 'Mind if I have a go first?'

Wendy saw her brother's face fall and she felt more and more angry. 'John's very good at it now, Father.'

'I'll be the judge of that, thank you, Wendy.' He stared at his daughter's pinched white face. What on earth was wrong with the child? She looked as if she loathed him. Really, these children were getting completely out of hand.

'Me! Me!' cried Michael. 'I want to sail John's boat!'

Mr Darling smiled indulgently at his youngest child. 'Come along, then, Michael. I'll show you.'

'But, Father –' John's face went red and he looked away.

Mr Darling didn't notice a thing. He took Michael's hand and led him towards the edge of the pond.

John chewed his lips and clenched his teeth, but it didn't make any difference. He started to cry.

'Shall I take the children home, ma'am?' asked Nanny Holborn as she heaved herself up from her stool. She threw a sideways look at John. 'I'd say they're rather tired.'

'John isn't tired, Mother,' said Wendy. 'He's upset. He's been hoping to show Father how he can sail his boat for weeks.'

'He's *tired*, ma'am,' said Nanny Holborn in a thin, dangerous voice.

Mrs Darling put her arm around John's shoulder. 'Would you like to go home, dear?'

John shook his head but couldn't speak.

'It's such a lovely day, Nanny,' said Mrs Darling lightly. For the first time, she noticed that Nanny Holborn had rather unpleasant tin-coloured eyes. 'I'll stay with John for a few more minutes.'

A hole opened in Wendy's stomach. That left her alone with Nanny Holborn, whom she had just contradicted in front of her mother.

At that moment, Esther Cunningham appeared in front of them in a pleated lilac dress, holding a frilly white parasol. She looked fresh and pretty and pleased to be out walking on such a lovely day. Wendy could have shouted for joy. Now she was going to make sure that Esther would rescue her.

'Mrs Darling! What a perfect day for a picnic!' Then Esther noticed everyone's uncomfortable faces. 'But I see you're just leaving.'

'No, we're not!' blurted Wendy.

'That's a pity,' said Esther. She smiled at Wendy. 'I had hoped you'd be able to walk home with me.'

'I'd love to.'

Esther looked puzzled. 'Are you sure? It's such a lovely day.'

'Positive,' said Wendy, ignoring Nanny Holborn's hot metal eyes. 'May, I, Mother?'

'Of course, dear.' Mrs Darling turned to see Michael and Mr Darling walking towards them. Michael's trousers hung limply around his knees. 'Oh dear, poor Michael,' she cried in her vague silvery voice. She turned to Nanny Holborn and something in her voice changed. 'But there is no sense punishing a child for an accident, don't you think?'

Nanny Holborn pressed her lips together and said nothing.

She knows, thought Wendy in amazement. *But who could have told her?*

* * *

'I wanted to make sure you were feeling better,' said Esther after they had walked for a few moments without speaking. When Letitia had gleefully told her about their game, Esther had been horrified. She was sure it wasn't normal for a young girl to know about such matters, let alone take such an unnatural interest in them. No wonder Wendy had been sick.

A thought had been bouncing back and forth like a shuttlecock in Wendy's head. On the one hand, Esther was the only person she could possibly confide in. On the other, Wendy knew that Esther was very fond of her father, and if she told her what happened, it would only make her unhappy, and while Letitia wouldn't know the reason, she would be delighted to see Esther upset. Wendy couldn't do it.

'It was an infection,' she said firmly. 'I get them sometimes.'

'Nothing to do with Letitia?'

'Letitia makes me feel stupid.' At least she could tell Esther half the truth. 'Anyway, she always pretends she knows more than me.' Wendy scuffed her black boots on the path. 'I don't really understand why we're friends. We don't have anything in common.'

'Are John and Henry friends?'

'Not really. John goes along with Henry's games.'

'What kinds of games?' asked Esther reluctantly.

'Last time Henry tied John to a chair and waved a red-hot poker in his face.' She looked up. 'He didn't hurt him though.'

'Dear Lord,' cried Esther. 'That's dreadful. Did John tell anyone?'

Wendy shook her head. 'Henry says worse things than that happen at his school. He says he's doing John a favour.'

'Don't you have other friends you play with?'

'Not really. Nanny says there are three of us and three's a crowd so we don't need anyone else in the nursery.' Wendy looked up. 'Anyway, mostly Nanny doesn't like other children.'

'Why on earth not?'

'She says they've got worms.'

Esther couldn't believe what she was hearing. Yet she knew to interfere was inconceivable. 'Why does she let you play with Letitia and Henry, then?'

'Because Mother thinks they're our best friends. That's what Lady Cunningham says anyway.'

Suddenly it occurred to Wendy that there might be a way to stop her father from spending time with Lady Cunningham. If the children didn't see each other then perhaps the adults wouldn't either. 'So, you see, there's not much point in us playing with Henry and Letitia any more.'

'I can understand that.'

Wendy ran her tongue around her lips. This was

more difficult than she thought. 'But I'd hate not to see you, Esther.' She went bright red. 'I think about you an awful lot. You're the only one who doesn't make me feel peculiar for reading books and stuff.'

To Wendy's horror, Esther stopped and bent down beside her. 'What's wrong?' she asked.

Wendy stared at the ground. She thought she'd been so clever. Now she had almost given herself away. 'Nothing. Nothing's wrong.'

'I hope not.' Esther stood up. 'Well, you won't be seeing Henry and Letitia for some time, so that should cheer you up.'

'You don't think I'm rude, do you?' asked Wendy uncomfortably.

'Certainly not. Given the circumstances, I think you've been remarkably restrained.' Esther laughed and ruffled Wendy's hair. 'Henry and Letitia are going to Northumberland tomorrow.'

'Is that the house called Saundersbane?'

Esther nodded. 'I expect Letitia has already told you how much she hates it.'

'She said it was dark and muddy and haunted by a wolf.'

'Haunted by a wolf?' Esther laughed and shook her head. 'Would it surprise you if I said that Letitia has never been to Saundersbane?'

Wendy shook her head. She was thinking about something else. If Letitia was in Northumberland, perhaps her mother had gone too. 'Are they all there?'

'Everyone except Papa. And they absolutely hate the country.' Esther grinned. 'But Papa insisted. Anyway, that means I've got him to myself for two months, so it couldn't be better.' She touched Wendy's cheek. 'But that's a secret, so you must promise not to tell anyone else.'

'May I ask you a question?'

'Go ahead.'

'How old were you when your mother died?'

'Younger than you. The only good thing about it was that I got to spend lots of time with my father.' Esther shrugged. 'It's different now.'

And Wendy knew from her voice that Esther hated Lady Cunningham as much as she did.

5

When Liza opened the front door, Mrs Darling walked in with an armful of parcels. 'Did you have a good shopping trip, ma'am?' she asked as she took the parcels.

'Very enjoyable, thank you,' replied Mrs Darling, her eyes shining. 'Selfridges is quite the most extraordinary place. It's like a whole town in one building. Is Mr Darling in?'

'Master's reading the paper in his study.'

Mrs Darling took off her coat and unpinned her wide-brimmed straw hat. 'I bought presents for everyone. Even me. Where are the children?'

'In the garden.' Liza was furious. Not only had Nanny Holborn kept the children inside for most of the day, she had especially asked Mrs Jenkins to make John's least favourite tea. Something about him not folding his socks properly before he put them in his shoes. 'Nanny

Holborn has just ordered bacon pie for their tea.'

'Bacon pie!' exclaimed Mrs Darling. 'What nonsense! Nanny knows very well that John hates cold bacon. Run along and tell Mrs Jenkins the children may have a cake for tea today.'

At that moment, the study door opened and George Darling stepped into the hall. He glared first at the mound of parcels, then he clicked his tongue and slammed his study door shut.

As Liza turned into the back passage, she heard Mr Darling's voice. 'Have you got a moment, my dear?' The words should have sounded quaint and courteous, but they didn't. They sounded harsh and sarcastic, as if he was so angry he could barely speak. Liza closed the passage door behind her. She didn't want to hear any more.

'It's for you,' said Mrs Darling.

George Darling stared at the silver and pearl tie pin

that glittered in a black velvet box. He said, 'I'm afraid you'll have to take it back.'

Mrs Darling's face froze. 'I can't. I put it on the account.'

'I told you two weeks ago not to use any of the accounts.' George Darling shook his head as if he was talking to a naughty child. 'And what do you do? You spend the afternoon buying presents for the children at Selfridges.'

'And for you, dear.' Mrs Darling reached out to touch her husband's hand. 'Surely you're not jealous.'

'Of course I'm not jealous,' snapped Mr Darling. 'For God's sake, your brain's no better than scrambled eggs.'

'I don't know what's got into you,' cried Mrs Darling, completely taken aback by her husband's tone of voice. 'Whenever you open your mouth these days, it's to say something nasty.' Suddenly she had had enough of pandering to his idiotic, unpleasant behaviour. His antics at the picnic in the park had been unforgivable. She watched him pour himself a glass of whisky from a decanter on the sideboard. 'Do you realise it is only four o'clock in the afternoon?'

'It's as good a time as any, as far as I'm concerned.' He tipped the contents of the glass down his throat and poured himself another.

Mrs Darling sat on the arm of a leather armchair. 'What is the matter?' she asked, as calmly as she could manage.

Her husband went over to his desk and brandished a pile of household account books in the air. 'I have already told you what the matter is. But do you listen?' He threw the books onto the floor. 'The butcher. The greengrocer. The fishmonger. The flower shop. Your dressmaker. The livery stable. Not one up to date. Money owing on every one.' He glared at his wife. 'I thought that you were capable of looking after the household bills at least. It seems I was wrong.'

Mrs Darling felt flustered and her mind shrank from the ostrich feather fan she had bought that afternoon. It had cost just under ten guineas – almost as much as Liza's yearly wage. The truth was, she had no memory of a discussion about money. How could she? He'd been behaving so badly, it was hardly surprising her mind was on other things. Besides, it was awfully difficult to take in what he told her, because frankly she really wasn't *interested.*

To Mrs Darling, money was like spring water bubbling out of the ground. She had no idea where it came from but it was always there. She didn't even know how to say what she wanted to ask. 'Are we, er, financially embarrassed, George?'

'We *were* financially embarrassed. Now we're broke.'

'What do you mean?'

Mr Darling laughed into his wife's puzzled face. 'We have no money left, dear.'

'But the, ah, the stock market . . . ' Mrs Darling said the words like a magical incantation. She had no idea what they meant.

'The stock market goes up and down. Two weeks ago it plummeted and it's going to take a long time to recover.'

This was even more confusing to Mrs Darling. The stock market was a pot of gold, and from time to time you went there and filled your pockets from it. 'But our . . . investments?'

'Of course we have investments. They're just not worth anything.'

George Darling stared at his wife's beautiful, infantile face. Blast it, had she never grown up? Victoria Cunningham's dark, clever features loomed in his mind. Now there was a woman . . . But in the same moment, he knew perfectly well that money was what she was interested in and that if she ever found out about his circumstances their affair would be over. Suddenly he felt overwhelmed by the disaster his life had become. He sat down and slumped forwards onto his desk.

'I don't understand,' Mrs Darling said hopelessly.

'There's nothing to understand,' muttered Mr Darling with his head in his arms. 'I've run out of luck. That's all there is to it.'

Mrs Darling stared at her husband's thick black hair. It glinted in a ray of sunshine that gleamed through the window. She thought of another sunny afternoon many years ago in her father's study at Rosegrove. 'Have him, if you can't wait,' her father had said. 'But you'll need to get used to living on luck, not land or bricks and mortar.'

But of course she had had to have him. He was so elegant and so charming. He had given her a diamond heart pierced with a silver arrow. He had driven her around

London in a shiny brougham filled with lilies. And he had promised her a life as magical as a fairy tale. She would never have to worry about anything, ever. She was his princess. How could she say no?

A handle clicked shut. Mrs Darling sat up with a jolt and found herself alone in the room. She heard the front door open and close.

Liza stood nervously in the doorway. 'Master says to inform you that he'll be at his club for the evening.' She bobbed and went away.

Mrs Darling looked down at the black household books that lay all over the floor and burst into tears.

'Do you think Nanny wears false teeth, Wendy?' John looked up from his *Boy's Own Paper*. He was pink and sweaty under his straw hat.

'Probably,' said Wendy. She was imagining that she had torn off her thick stockings and ripped up her stupid flounced dress and was now lying in the sun in her slip and knickers. 'Or actually she grows new ones like a crocodile.'

She wriggled about on the tartan rug and made jaw-snapping movements with her hands. Beside her Nana lifted up her head and yawned.

Rubbish and unkind to crocodiles.

'I know it's rubbish,' said Wendy. She tickled Nana's ears. 'And you're right about crocodiles, of course. But it's all right for you, you can stick your tongue out when it's hot. What am I supposed to do?'

Sweat.

'I'm doing that already, thank you very much.'

'*Please,* Wendy! Stop talking to Nana!' cried John. 'Do you or don't you think Nanny wears false teeth?'

Wendy crammed her hat on her head and sat up. 'Why? What difference would it make if she did?'

'Because if they're made of vulcanite we could sell them for 4d and if they're silver we could get 9d. And if

Mrs Jenkins wears them, we could sell hers too.' He pointed to the advertisement in the magazine. 'It says here that condition doesn't matter.'

'Quite so,' said Wendy, as if selling false teeth was something she thought about every day. 'But the thing is, I wouldn't ever steal anything from Mrs Jenkins because she's one of the only grown-ups in our house I happen to admire. So that leaves us with 9d at the most. And I would want more than that to go fishing around in Nanny's awful mouth.'

'How about if we tied her up first?' said John hopefully. 'Henry lent me a book of knots and there's some rope in the garden shed.'

Wendy flapped her arms. 'Ever seen a pig fly?'

'Oh, shut up.'

'Look, if you really need some money, I've got some saved up.'

'You mean pocket money?' asked John crossly.

'What other kind is there?'

'It still won't be enough.'

'Enough for what?'

'Enough to pay our train fare so we can run away and stay with Uncle Arthur,' said John. His pink face turned red and angry. 'I don't understand it, Wendy! We always go to Rosegrove for the summer. But now it's over halfway through and we're still stuck here in this stupid garden, on this stupid rug. We don't even have a sandpit because Father says cats go to the lavatory in them.'

'Why are you looking so cross?' asked Michael, marching up with a wooden soldier in his hand. 'Is it because I'm going to die?'

'Don't be silly, Michael,' said Wendy. 'John's not cross. He's just fed up with being hot and stuck in London. Anyway, who's been telling you you're going to die?'

'Nanny has,' said Michael solemnly. He pointed across the garden to where Nanny Holborn was sitting under a sunshade, jabbing viciously at a piece of crochet. 'She says that boys who join the army when they grow up always die.' His lower lip began to tremble. 'And Father says I'm to be a soldier.' He held up the painted wooden soldier in his hands. 'That's why he gave me this for my birthday.' A big fat tear wobbled down Michael's cheek. 'I don't want to be a soldier.'

'I want to go to Rosegrove,' said John, gouging out a hole in the grass.

'Me too,' sniffed Michael.

'Look here,' said Wendy crossly, although she wasn't feeling cross. In fact, she felt as tearful as Michael and as furious as John. But she was the oldest and somehow they had to make the best of it. What else could they do? 'Michael, don't listen to what Father says. He's not himself at the moment. I heard Mother say so. And John –'

Wendy ran out of steam. She also desperately wanted to get away from London. For weeks the weather had been getting hotter and hotter, and Nanny Holborn had been getting more and more bad-tempered. No matter how hard they tried to please her, she could always find some reason to explode into a rage and march them up to the nursery. In the past ten days, Wendy had spent six afternoons lying on her bed, not even allowed her books to read. And all she did was worry. About her father, mostly. He was so different nowadays: pasty, haggard and snappish all the time. Yesterday she had been curled up on the rug in the garden, talking to Nana, and her father had suddenly appeared beside her. When she looked up, he didn't speak, he just stared at her. Something was wrong and it was nothing to do with Lady Cunningham, because she was still away in Northumberland. Even her mother seemed to have given up and barely spoke to him.

'Stop thinking!' wailed Michael, prodding her with his soldier.

'Why should I?' Wendy almost shouted.

Michael's face crumpled.

'Sorry, titch, it's not your fault,' said Wendy. 'I want to get out of here as much as you two do.'

Michael pushed his face into Wendy's. 'What were you thinking about then?'

'Father.'

'I call that a damned bad show,' said Michael solemnly. 'That's what Father said to me when I tried to sail John's boat.'

'Father doesn't like us any more,' said John flatly. 'Mother doesn't care either. I heard them talking and she said, "What's the point of keeping them?" '

'John! For heaven's sake!' Wendy slid her eyes sideways towards Michael, who was looking horrified. 'You must have got it wrong. What she must have said was, "What's the point of keeping them *here*?" They were talking about Rosegrove. Mother wants us to go.'

'Then why can't we?'

'How should I know?' said Wendy.

'Then we'll have to pinch some teeth,' said John. 'Platinum ones are 2s 6d.'

'Good idea,' said Wendy. 'And when you tie up Nanny, do me a favour and use lots of rope and a different kind of knot.'

'So she swings, you mean?'

'Something like that. It might even shake out her teeth.'

'Nanny doesn't like swinging,' said Michael. 'Anyway, she keeps her teeth in a box. I saw them.'

'Aha!' said John, looking up. 'What were they made of?'

'Teeth!' cried Michael proudly.

'Oh, for goodness' *sake,*' said John, and they all rolled around the rug laughing.

Across the lawn, Nanny Holborn's head jerked round. She didn't approve of children laughing like that. It sounded rude and out of control. As she watched, they began to laugh harder, peering into each other's mouths. *Like a group of dirty monkeys,* she thought, trying to ignore the hot, sweaty itch under her vast shelf of bosom. It was ridiculous to be outside in this heat. If she hadn't run into Mrs Darling that morning, she would have kept the children inside. She ran her tongue around her lips and made an angry *tschh* noise. Her blue uniform was tight and uncomfortable, and her black lace-up boots felt two sizes too small. Why should she sit roasting in the sun for the sake of three badly behaved children? Fury surged through her. She snatched up the tapestry bag at her feet and stuffed her crochet hooks inside it. At that moment, Liza appeared with a tray. On it were three glasses and a pitcher.

'Lemonade, children!' Liza called.

Wendy and John jumped to their feet and ran cheering across the grass. Mrs Jenkins's lemonade was one of their favourite treats.

'Goodness, what a scorcher!' said Liza, putting the tray down on the table.

Nanny Holborn rose to her feet.

'Take that muck back to the kitchen! No one gives the children food or drink without asking me first.'

'Please, Nanny!' cried John. 'It's so hot!'

'And we're *so* thirsty,' said Michael. Nanny turned her crazy tin-coloured eyes on him. He looked nervously at his sister. 'Aren't we, Wendy?'

The lemonade jug had come from Rosegrove. It was yellow and had daisies painted on the sides. Inside Wendy could see sprigs of mint floating on top of the lemonade. The sharp lemony smell almost made her drool. 'Please, Nanny,' said Wendy with as much control as she could manage. 'It would only be polite. Mrs Jenkins made it specially.'

'I don't care who made it! You are not drinking it,' snapped Nanny Holborn. She raised her hand and Wendy dodged away from the table. 'Lemons upset the stomach.'

'Poppycock!' cried a furious voice, and Mrs Jenkins strode onto the terrace. Her face was flushed and the sleeves of her blouse were rolled up to her elbows. She looked square and strong and extremely angry. 'The children are thirsty. They have had nothing to drink since lunch time.'

Nanny Holborn shot Liza a vicious glance. 'How do you know? Has Little Miss Nosy Parker been telling tales again?'

'Control yourself, Nanny Holborn,' cried Mrs Jenkins in a shocked voice.

'I will not be spied on in my own nursery,' snarled Nanny Holborn.

'Then perhaps you should carry out your duties differently.'

And in that instant Wendy knew how her mother had found out about Michael. Mrs Jenkins had told her.

The two women glared at each other. Wendy could

feel the hatred crackling between them like lightning. Instinctively she stepped backwards. Out of the corner of her eye, she saw that Michael had taken fright and hidden under a chair. Only John stood still, his mouth a round dark O in his face.

'I am responsible for these children,' said Nanny Holborn coldly. 'And I do not take my orders from you.'

'What the children eat is my responsibility,' said Mrs Jenkins. 'What's more, being cooped up indoors is not good for them.'

'I'll see you put out on the street for this,' hissed Nanny Holborn at Liza. She turned towards Wendy and John. 'Come along this minute. Up to the nursery with you.'

John stared at the lemonade, not moving. 'I'm thirsty,' he said stubbornly.

'Do as you're told,' bellowed Nanny Holborn.

She reached out to pull him by the collar, but he

ducked. She grabbed Wendy instead, grinding her bony fingers into her arm. Wendy screamed.

Something snapped in Liza's mind. 'Take your hands off her, you miserable old bitch,' she shouted in a high, shrill voice.

'Liza!' cried Mrs Jenkins. 'For heaven's sake, girl!'

But Liza couldn't bear it one more moment. 'She hits them, Mrs Jenkins. She makes them drink castor oil for no reason.' Her voice was breaking with angry sobs. 'She hits them. I know she does.'

Nobody spoke. A blackbird sang in the chestnut tree. Far away, two dogs started barking. John and Wendy stared at each other. Each knew what the other was thinking. *What would happen once they were alone with Nanny Holborn in the nursery?*

Something made Wendy look up. Her mother was standing at her bedroom window, her face white and smooth as a doll's. As she watched, her mother stepped back and pulled the curtain across.

Mrs Jenkins had seen her too.

Nanny Holborn had her back to the house. She pulled herself up to her full height and glared at Liza. 'The mistress will deal with you,' she said in a thin, poisonous voice.

Liza let out a cry that was somewhere between fury and despair. She picked up the jug of lemonade and threw it at Nanny Holborn's chest as hard as she could. The jug hit the stone terrace with a crash and broke into a hundred yellow pieces. Liza ran sobbing down the stone stairs and into the kitchen.

The French windows opened and Mrs Darling walked onto the terrace, ghostly in a flowing muslin dress, her face still as marble. Wendy fought off an almost overwhelming urge to run and wrap her arms around her mother's waist. But she knew she must stand and wait until her mother had spoken.

'Mrs Jenkins, you will kindly ask Alice Jameson to

give the children their tea this afternoon in order that Nanny Holborn may recover herself.'

Wendy couldn't believe her ears. Her mother's voice was cold and calm, as if the sight of Nanny Holborn purple with fury and dripping with lemonade was nothing out of the ordinary.

A muscle twitched in Nanny Holborn's face. Wendy stood rigid, expecting her to explode. Instead she was completely still, as if she had been turned into stone.

On the other side of the terrace, Mrs Jenkins was staring at her feet to hide the look of triumph on her face. She curtsied and said, 'Come with me, children.'

She marched past Nanny Holborn to where Michael was still cowering under his chair. At the sight of Mrs Jenkins bending down towards him, he crawled out and held her tightly by the hand. Then, looking firmly away from Nanny Holborn's frozen face, he allowed himself to be led back across the terrace.

'Mrs Jenkins,' Mrs Darling said, turning as she stepped lightly back through the French windows. 'Send Liza to see me immediately, please.'

'Yes, ma'am.'

It wasn't until then that Wendy realised her mother hadn't once even looked at Nanny Holborn.

In the nursery, Alice Jameson threw away the bacon pie and cut the children thick slices of bread and honey, and told them stories about growing up in Scotland, where her father was a fisherman and caught hundreds of silvery fish in his net.

Michael was delighted with Alice's stories. He was too young to understand what had happened that afternoon. He got down off his chair and climbed onto Alice's lap. 'I caught a whale once, Alice.'

'Where was that, dear?'

'In the Round Pond. It was this big.' He held his hands wide apart and waved his sandwich in the air. Part of it fell, sticky side down, on the floor.

Wendy and John looked nervously at each other. Nanny Holborn would have smacked Michael on the side of the head, called him a filthy little brute and made him eat it.

But Alice only laughed. She picked up the bread and fed it to Nana, who was lying under the table.

Wendy watched as Nana gobbled up the sticky bread.

I could get used to this.

'So could I,' said Wendy out loud.

Alice looked puzzled, then she smiled and buttered another piece of bread.

Later Wendy and John lay in their beds and watched the curtains flutter in the warm summer breeze. They had gone to bed early. It seemed easier that way. In the far corner of the night nursery, Michael had fallen asleep the moment Alice had tucked him into bed.

Nana lay on the floor by Wendy's bed. 'Of course she can stay with you,' Alice had said. 'When I was young, my wee dog slept with me every night.'

John kicked off his sheet and let one of his legs dangle out of the side of his bed. 'Do you think Mother will send Liza away?'

Wendy thought for a moment. Her mother hadn't sounded cross with Liza. But then, she hadn't sounded cross with Nanny Holborn either. The more Wendy thought about it, the more she realised that what she had seen on the terrace was a battle between Mrs Jenkins and Nanny Holborn. 'I don't know,' she said. 'But if Nanny Holborn comes back, then Liza can't stay. Not after what she said.'

'I hope Nanny Holborn dies in the night,' said John viciously.

'Don't count your chickens.'

They lay still for a moment and listened hard for a

creak on the linoleum floor. There was nothing, only the endless clip-clopping of horses' hooves and the grinding of a barrel organ far away in the distance.

'Do you think Mother heard what Liza said?'

'Mother heard everything.'

Bedsprings twanged. 'How do you know?'

'I saw her. She was standing at the bedroom window. That's why she came down.'

'Then she'll *have* to send Nanny Holborn away,' said John.

'What makes you think that?'

'Because now she knows the truth. She can't pretend we're happy anymore.'

'But why should Mother believe Liza?' asked Wendy. 'Nanny Holborn could be denying everything right now. Anyway, Mother always asks Father before she does anything.'

'Father doesn't care who looks after us as long as

he gets what he wants,' said John, who still hadn't forgiven his father for choosing Michael and not him to sail his boat on the pond.

A door slammed down the corridor. Both children froze in their beds, waiting to hear the familiar dreadful thud of Nanny Holborn's boots. But there was nothing.

Wendy inched back under her bedclothes so the bedsprings wouldn't twang. Beside her, John did the same. As if by agreement, neither of them spoke again. As Wendy drifted into a fitful sleep, she dreamed of the sock full of pennies Liza kept in her room. One day she had shown it to Wendy. 'Half as much again,' she'd said, 'and it's Mrs Charlie Pickles for me.' The thought of Nanny Holborn made Wendy groan out loud. She reached down and felt for Nana's head on the floor.

'What will we do if she comes back? We'll be all on our own.'

Go to sleep. You'll make yourself sick with your worrying.

Wendy

* * *

Mrs Darling sat in her dressing room and stared at a leather jewellery box. She closed her eyes. *They had been married for two months. It was a beautiful spring day in April. A walk in Hyde Park to look at the daffodils, an empty bench, the box passing from his hands to hers. A string of ten opals, each one surrounded by diamonds, each end fastened to two white taffeta ribbons which tied at the back. My dearest, I shall love you for ever.*

She opened her eyes and looked down at the box. A receipt from a pawn shop in Covent Garden for £215 10s – *Take it or leave it, dearie. I ain't no charity* – folded neatly underneath a pile of banknotes. A small cloth bag held a handful of coins.

She counted out ten guineas, put the bag back in the box and put the box in the middle drawer of her dressing table.

Then she waited for her husband to come home.

* * *

The last of the afternoon sun shone through the yellow panes in the stained-glass windows. It bounced off the gold frames of the portraits on the walls and settled in glowing pools on the Turkish carpets. Mrs Darling leaned forwards and rested her arm on the end of the carved wooden sofa.

Across the room, her husband sat down at his desk and began writing quickly on a piece of paper. 'I'm sorry,' he said, 'but we will have to do without Nanny Holborn as from tomorrow.'

'But how did you know?'

'Know what?'

Mrs Darling shook her head. 'Her conduct in the nursery.'

Mr Darling looked puzzled. 'Her conduct seems perfectly satisfactory to me. It's her wages I'm talking about. We can't afford 'em.'

A water cart splashed and rattled in the street. Children shouted excitedly.

'Then we're agreed,' said Mrs Darling. 'The sooner she goes the better. Liza will look after the children for the time being.'

For a moment Mr Darling felt entirely confused. He hadn't expected his wife to be so understanding. 'I'm sorry, my dear. These are difficult times for all of us.'

'Yes.'

'And, of course, we must make every effort to be discreet.'

'Quite.' Mrs Darling spread her fingers and gazed absent-mindedly at her rings. 'Which is why I am sending the children to Rosegrove tomorrow.'

Mr Darling stared at her as if she was mad. 'Don't you understand? I cannot possibly afford to send the children to Rosegrove.' He folded Nanny Holborn's letter of dismissal and put it into an envelope. 'However pleased I might be to see the back of them.'

Mrs Darling stood up. As every day passed, it

seemed more and more that her life was happening not to her but to someone who stood just behind her shoulder.

'You needn't concern yourself with the money,' she said, without looking at him. 'I have taken care of the arrangements.'

Mr Darling opened his mouth to ask how, then shut it. He didn't want to know.

A carriage clock chimed on the mantelpiece. As she turned the handle of the door, Mrs Darling wondered idly what it might fetch.

6

'Charlie is my darling! Charlie is my dear!' sang Liza, high and clear. There was a rattle of teacups and the sound of plates being laid on a table.

Wendy opened her eyes. Probably she was still dreaming. But how could she be dreaming when the curtains were open and the room smelled of fresh bread?

'Charlie! Charlie! Give me your answer do! I'm half crazy all for the love of you.'

One thought went round and round in Wendy's mind. The more she thought it, the bigger it got until it became a huge aching hope that soared out of the window and turned into something as big and light as a hot-air balloon. *Nanny Holborn has left. Nanny Holborn has left. NANNY HOLBORN HAS LEFT!*

She jumped out of bed without putting on her dressing gown and slippers and yanked open the door to the nursery.

'Good morning, Wendy!' Liza was standing by the table, putting out the napkins. But it was a Liza Wendy had never seen before. Her brown hair was pulled back in a soft bun and she wore a bright blue jacket and a high-necked white blouse tucked into a red skirt. She laughed at Wendy's open-mouthed face. 'Don't you know it's rude to stare?'

Wendy made herself look carefully around the room. *Look for clues,* she told herself. *It's the only way to know for sure. Grown-ups will tell you anything to shut you up.*

But it was all right. There were clues everywhere. Someone had picked a bunch of flowers from the garden and put them in a vase on the table. Someone had put out a jar of jam as well as a jar of honey. There was a new crusty loaf of bread that sat on the wooden board, waiting to be cut. There was no sign of the usual stale half-loaf from the day before that had to be finished first. But the biggest clue of all was that the feeling in the nursery was completely different.

Wendy looked over to the corner, where Nana was sitting in her basket.

Go on. Ask her.

Even though she was afraid that just mentioning the name might break the spell, Wendy said, 'Has Nanny Holborn left?'

Liza nodded.

'Did she leave us a goodbye letter?'

'She didn't say goodbye to anyone. She was already gone when Alice got up at six.'

Wendy fought back a mad urge to cry. Even though she hated her, Nanny Holborn had looked after Wendy since she was a baby. The idea of her leaving the house she had lived in for so long, on her own and with no one to say goodbye to her was horribly sad.

Liza bent down and put her hands on Wendy's shoulders. 'She won't be on her own, Wendy. She has a sister in Peckham. Her trunk is following her there today.'

'She was so mean to us, Liza.'

'I know, dear. But she's gone, so what's the point in thinking about her?'

'Did Mother send her away or did she ask Father first?'

'I don't know and it doesn't matter now.' There was no way Liza could tell Wendy what Mrs Jenkins had said – that Nanny Holborn's sacking could not have had anything to do with how she had treated the children because Mr Darling had given her a good reference for her next employers. *Truth is, Liza, Master's got money worries. But it was a convenience all round, since the Mistress had already given her her marching orders. She told me so herself.*

Liza began to cut the bread into thick, squashy slices. 'Look, Wendy, when I went to see your mother, I was expecting . . . well, I didn't know what I was expecting. But she never mentioned Nanny Holborn. And she didn't mention the jug I broke either. She just asked me if I would be able to stay on and look after you.' Liza smiled. 'Will that keep you quiet?'

Wendy couldn't believe her ears. 'You mean we're not going to have a proper nanny?'

'Only little me,' said Liza. 'For the rest of the summer, anyway, and Alice is to help me with you.'

Wendy was too flabbergasted to speak. It was the best thing that could have happened.

Nana lifted her head.

I told you not to worry.

'Aren't you pleased?' asked Liza.

Wendy threw her arms around Liza's waist. 'I'm so happy I think I'm going to burst.'

Liza laughed. 'In that case you'd better hold on to your belly, because we're leaving for Rosegrove this morning and Nana's coming too!'

Two hours later, Wendy knocked on her mother's door,

wearing her best summer dress made of thick cotton with feather-stitching on the collar. She waited for a moment, then she knocked again and went inside.

'Did you want to see me, Mother?' Wendy tried hard to keep the impatience out of her voice. Everyone else was on the pavement, waiting for the bus, and she wanted to be with them.

Her mother was standing at her window, looking down at the street. As she turned, Wendy could see that she had been crying.

'I wanted to talk to you before you left,' said Mrs Darling in a squeezed voice.

Wendy stared. 'Aren't you coming with us?'

'No.' Mrs Darling swallowed. 'That's why I wanted to talk to you.' She took a deep breath. 'It's about Nanny Holborn.'

'You're not going to ask her back, are you?'

Mrs Darling started at her daughter's voice and felt

her throat tighten. If only she had spent more time with the children. But how could she, when her husband was such a child himself? 'No, I am not going to ask her back.' She put her arms around her daughter's shoulders. 'I only wish you had told me about her before.'

You wouldn't have believed me, said Wendy to herself. *You only believed Mrs Jenkins because she was a grown-up.* She stared uncomfortably at her feet. What was the point of making her mother more upset by telling her the truth? The best thing to do was change the subject. 'Liza said we aren't having another nanny for the rest of the summer.'

'That's true. And I wanted to ask you to be extra good at Rosegrove and to make sure the boys mind their manners with Liza and to be a help when you can. Especially with Michael.'

'Of course I will, Mother,' said Wendy proudly. It was the first time her mother had asked for help. 'I'll have Michael reading by the time you come down.'

'That's the other thing. I might not come down. Or not to stay anyway, just to bring you all home.'

'But you always come down to Rosegrove.'

'Some things change, Wendy. You'll learn that one day.' Mrs Darling sighed. 'Anyway, it all depends on your father.'

Wendy realised that she hadn't thought of her father all morning and had completely forgotten that she would have to say goodbye to him. 'But Father stays in London and works all summer.' He'd told her as much time and time again. Her mother looked pale and tired. 'I think you should come, Mother. Father can look after himself.'

Mrs Darling laughed, but it didn't sound right. 'Your father needs to be looked after too, dear.'

John's voice rose from the pavement. 'Quick, Liza, Wendy! The bus is coming!'

'Wendy! Wendy! Wendy!' shouted Michael.

Wendy ran to the door. 'Where's Father? I must say goodbye.' For a moment, she had forgotten everything except the excitement of going away. Then she stopped, because she remembered what went on in the house every day. 'He's not here, is he?'

Her mother shook her head. 'I'm sorry, dear. He – he went out early –'

'He forgot all about us because he's at his club,' said Wendy angrily. Then she went bright red. She had said too much.

This time, Mrs Darling did not try to hide the tears in her eyes. 'I'm sorry, sugar mouse. I'm so sorry. He's got a lot on his mind. I know it's difficult –'

'Where's Wendy?' yelled John from below.

Wendy ran across the room and stuck her head out of the window. A horse-drawn bus was waiting on the cobbles. Liza and the footman were busy handing parcels and bags up to the driver. Nana stood with Michael on the pavement. 'Coming!' shouted Wendy. She pulled her mother by the hand. 'Say goodbye to us, Mother.'

For a split second Mrs Darling didn't move, then she spoke in an odd, choky voice. 'Wendy, I –'

'You don't want John and Michael to see you crying, do you?'

Mrs Darling wiped at her eyes with her lace handkerchief. 'It's silly, I know.'

'Come on, Mother. John and Michael won't care. They probably won't even notice. But if you don't say goodbye, they'll be very sad.' She tugged her mother's arm and felt her give way. She led her across the room and down the stairs.

Wendy gripped the seat in front of her. She was glad they had been allowed to sit on top of the bus. All the noise and the crazy traffic had almost wiped away the memory of the sadness on her mother's face.

'Watch out,' shouted John.

The bus swerved away as a motor car roared past, missing a woman selling flowers by inches.

'That's Dora!' cried the driver from the high seat below them. 'I like to keep her on her toes! Now, hang on, young 'uns! This 'ere is Piccadilly Circus!'

'Yippee!' shouted John, and a huge grin split his face. 'I'm going to drive a bus, Wendy! I don't care what Father says.'

There was a great roar, as if they had been sucked into a whirlpool. Engines clattered, horses snorted and carriages and motor cars of every description swirled around in a circle. Time and time again, Wendy's hand flew to her mouth as boys in flat caps weaved in and out of the traffic, inches away from being crushed to death.

'Shut your eyes if you don't like it,' yelled John.

'Who says I don't like it?' Wendy shouted back.

As the bus turned up Regent Street, John looked at

Wendy and burst out laughing. 'Your face is *filthy.*'

'So's yours,' cried Wendy.

John licked his finger and ran it down his cheek. 'I'll never wash again, ever.'

But Wendy didn't reply. She was staring at a window in a department store. Over it were written the words 'Swan & Edgar'. A huge swing was decorated like a maypole with ribbons and flowers. A girl in a pink dress swung backwards and forwards, pushed by a young man with a fixed grin and boater. Wendy knew that they were dummies worked by some sort of machine, but it looked so real! And she realised all of a sudden that they really, truly were on their way down to Rosegrove. Her yearning to be with Thomas again made her feel almost sick.

'Oxford Street,' cried the bus driver. 'Not long now.'

Wendy jabbed John in the ribs and pointed to the other side of the road.

A bus exactly like theirs was draped with a huge banner which said VOTES FOR WOMEN. It was absolutely packed with young women. They all wore straw hats and bright summer dresses and they laughed and chatted and waved tiny white banners.

'Suffragettes,' cried Liza. 'Cor, what a party!'

Wendy stared at the bus. The young women didn't look at all like the serious people she had imagined suffragettes to be. They looked more like friends on their way to an outing by the seaside.

As the two buses passed each other, someone waved a newspaper at them.

'Not me, sweetheart,' shouted their driver. 'I can't read. But my missus can.'

The woman laughed and threw the paper into the bus. 'Send her along and good luck to you!'

As Wendy looked at the smiling faces and the pretty dresses, she found herself staring at Esther

Cunningham. But it was an Esther she barely recognised. She was laughing and pointing to a policeman scowling on the pavement. The girl next door to her blew him a cheeky kiss and waved her white flag. Wendy was suddenly aware that she was grinning too. She looked again at the faces in the packed bus. They all had the same bright, kind, intelligent look as Esther. And then Esther saw her.

'Wendy!' she cried, her voice rising above the roar of the traffic.

As the buses jolted past each other, all Wendy could do was crane her head around and wave as hard as she could.

'Who was that?' asked Liza.

'Esther Cunningham,' said Wendy proudly.

'Never!' Liza turned and stared as the bus pulled away. 'Fancy! Miss Esther, chaining herself to railings and that!'

'Do you think it's wrong?'

'Me? I don't think anything about it. Live and let live, I say.'

Wendy threw back her head and snorted with laughter.

'Why are you laughing, then?' asked Liza.

'Do you really want to know?'

'I wouldn't have asked if I didn't.'

'I was just thinking that if Nanny Holborn had seen her she would have torn off her head and made her eat it.'

Liza laughed. 'You're right there, dearie.'

If the bus hadn't jerked forward at that moment, Wendy would have hugged her.

John's eyes were the size of dinner plates. He ran his hands along the plush button-backed seats and peered into the bottomless polish of the pedestal table. 'This is a first-class saloon, Wendy!' he said in an awed voice. '*First class!*'

'What if we drop crumbs?' whispered Michael, stroking the velvet walls as if they were alive.

'The guard comes and locks you in the luggage van,' said Wendy.

'Liar,' said Michael.

'Yup.'

Alice looked around the carriage and raised her eyebrows at Liza. 'This must have cost a fortune.' She lowered her voice. 'I thought you said –'

Liza shook her head quickly and shrugged. If Mr Darling wanted to spend his money on a first-class carriage, she wasn't about to complain.

Outside the window, there was a shrill whistle blast and the train shuddered forwards.

Wendy sank her teeth into the tiniest corner of her cheese sandwich and chewed as slowly as she could. She was determined to make it last the whole train journey. In her other hand, she held the stub of a pencil. She looked down at the picture of Rosegrove she was drawing for Alice. It wasn't her best drawing, because the train shook from side to side a lot and it was hard to concentrate when there was so much looking out of the window that had to be done.

As well as her drawing, she was playing a game with John where he got five points for every motor car he spotted and Wendy got three points for every horse and cart. So far, Wendy was winning easily, because, as the train rumbled through the suburbs and into the countryside, there was barely a motor car to be seen.

'That's nothing *like* Rosegrove,' said John, snatching the piece from in front of Wendy. 'Look, Alice, I'll show you!'

Wendy opened her mouth to protest, then she realised she couldn't be bothered. Even though all the ventilators were open, it was hot in the carriage. Now she wished she'd worn the loose pinafore Liza had put out for her.

The train swayed and rattled over the tracks. Gradually her pencil dropped from her hand. Her head nodded onto her chest. The carriage turned into a room. Thomas was sitting on the far side by the window. All she could see was the back of his head, but she knew from the size of his shoulders that he had grown. Suddenly she was frightened. He was fifteen now. Would he think she was too young to be his friend any more? She stared and stared, willing him to turn around. As soon as she saw him she would know the answer from the expression on his face. But he kept looking out of the window, and when at last she plucked up courage and began to speak to him, the words came out wrong – and people were laughing at her.

'Wake up, Wendy!' cried John. 'You were talking in your sleep.'

She shook her dream away. The yearning for Rosegrove was so strong, it was like a pain in her body. 'How long now?'

'Next station.' John peered at her. 'What's wrong? Did you have a nightmare or something?'

'I was dreaming about Thomas.'

'What about him?'

'I was wondering whether he'll be too grown up to want to be with me.'

John rolled his eyes. 'For goodness' sake, Wendy, we're going to Rosegrove! Stop worrying about everything!'

Wendy rubbed her hands over her face. 'Sorry. You're right. Do you think Nana's been given any water in the guard's van?'

John punched his sister on the arm. 'Shut up, will you?'

The station was the same. So was Jock, the coachman. His face still looked like old leather and his cheeks were still hidden under huge bushy side-whiskers. When he saw

Wendy, he didn't say, 'Are you keeping well?' or, 'How is your mother?' He just held out his hand to help her up into the wagonette and said, 'Hello, Miss Wendy,' as if he had seen her that morning, not last Christmas.

And she replied, 'I'm back, Jock. How's Brandy?'

Jock patted the rump of the glossy brown cob. 'Never better.' He turned to where Nana was sitting in the shade of the wheel. 'Come along, Nana. You don't want to be left behind, do you?'

Nana jumped in and sat herself by Wendy's feet.

'Poor Nana. You look hot and thirsty.'

Nana rested her head on her paws.

Some of us didn't travel first class.

Ten minutes later, as the wagonette trundled between the high hedges, Wendy breathed in the mustiness of the wheat fields and the sharp green smell of the woods. Jock held the reins loosely in his lap. He never seemed to tighten them, yet Brandy knew exactly where to go.

They stopped at a crossroads. Brandy turned his head to the left and to the right. Nobody was coming. He walked on. Jock winked at Wendy and the wagonette rolled down the lane.

Wendy loved the hedges in the country. They always looked as if they had been painted in two colours. The bottom three-quarters were white with dust thrown up by the wheels of farm carts. At the top, where it was too high for the dust to settle, a strip of brilliant green leaves sparkled in the sun.

'Terrible dusty this summer,' said Jock. 'Same as always.'

'Does Peggy know we're coming?' said John suddenly, as if the question had been on his mind for some time.

'Shouldn't we tell Uncle Arthur first?' asked Michael solemnly.

'Uncle Arthur *asked* us, idiot,' said Wendy.

'That's all right, then,' said Michael happily.

'Everyone knows you're coming, I should think, Master Michael.' Jock turned to Wendy. 'I haven't seen Thomas, of course, but Peggy's been talking about nothing else except Master John, till 'er tongue's fit to fall off.'

Brandy turned right between two stone pillars with acorns on top.

'Rosegrove Estate' was carved in gold letters on either side.

Wendy jumped down from the wagonette and, with Nana beside her, ran along the lane towards the field at the bottom of the house. She stood knee deep in wild flowers, gazing across the gardens at the house she had been longing to see all summer.

Rosegrove was like a black and white gingerbread palace. The huge wooden beams that made up the framework of the house were arranged in herringbone patterns and diamonds and clover leaves, the spaces in between filled with bright white plaster. The steep wooden eaves were so beautifully carved that they looked like strips of lace. She pulled off her straw hat and felt the warmth of the sun on her face and the magic of Rosegrove inside her. Aunt Emily and Uncle Arthur had no children, but whenever she came to the house it felt as if she was coming home to a family. In all the years she had been here, she had never overheard a single conversation in which someone said something bad about someone else. People seemed happy to get on with their lives. Wendy thought of the angry secrets piled up in every dark corner of her parents' house in London.

'It's like another world, Nana, isn't it?'

But Nana wasn't listening. She'd caught the scent of a rabbit.

Wendy bent down and began to pick handfuls of cornflowers. They were blue as the sky and shone in her hands.

Arthur Meredith looked up from the newspaper he was reading under a garden umbrella. He shaded his eyes and watched Wendy bend to pick what wild flowers were left in the heat of the summer: cornflowers probably. He was glad his sister had at last sent the children down to the country. And he was particularly fond of his niece. She was such a splendidly outspoken urchin of a child. And she had that golden hair and those blue eyes.

Actually, she reminded him of himself and her mother when they were children. The boys, on the other hand, were more like their father. Arthur found that difficult. No matter how much he tried, he couldn't warm to his brother-in-law. Frankly, he thought him a childish prig, always out to impress and with little or no imagination. His mind went back to their last conversation. They had been talking of the children's future. No mention of Wendy, of course. It was the boys George was concerned with. John was to join the Navy. Michael was to join the Guards. And that was that. He had no interest in any opinions they might have of their own. Arthur Meredith shook his head. The idiot seemed to think that life was a set of train tracks.

Hadn't he learned anything?

Wendy crawled on her hands and knees through the long grass. She had tucked her dress into her knickers so it didn't get covered in green stains. At first she was sure Uncle Arthur had seen her. This was a pity, because she had got down from the wagonette just after the gates so she could creep up on him and thrust her flowers in his face. Then, just as she was certain he had spotted her and she was about to get up and walk over towards him, he had looked away and hadn't turned around again. Now he was standing a few feet away from her. She crouched behind a low stone wall and stared at him.

Uncle Arthur. His white linen suit was crumpled as usual and his long fine-boned face was tanned and clean-shaven. Wendy was proud that her eyes were the same dark blue as his, even though his had a few more wrinkles around them than last time. She pulled her dress out of her knickers and jumped over the wall. 'Surprise!' she yelled, and burst out laughing when she saw the look on his face. She clutched him around the waist and breathed in his smell of sandalwood. There was no hint of hair oil or tobacco, like her father. And unlike her father, her uncle knew how to hug. He didn't just drape his arms around your neck and let them slip off a minute later. He hugged like a bear, till your ribs cracked and you knew you were at home with someone you loved.

'When are you going to grow?' It was what he always said.

'Never!' It was what she always replied. She hugged him again and told the picture in her mind of her father to go away and leave her alone.

'We had our own bus and our own carriage,' she cried. He sat down and she leaned on the arm of his chair. '*First class!*'

'That would please Nanny Holborn,' said Uncle Arthur, smiling.

'Nanny Holborn's gone.' Wendy touched an engraved gold cufflink with her finger. She looked straight into her uncle's dark blue eyes. It was almost like looking into her mother's eyes, except Mother usually looked away. Uncle Arthur never did. 'Mother sent her away.'

'It all sounds rather dramatic.' He watched Wendy's face. She looked tired and her gaiety sounded almost brittle. Arthur Meredith frowned to himself. His sister's last letter had been hectic and confused. Something was wrong in London and, whatever it was, it was affecting the girl. 'What happened?'

Wendy shrugged, as if it didn't matter. She could see her uncle was worried and she wished she had kept her mouth shut. 'Liza threw a jug at her.'

'Good Lord!' cried Arthur Meredith in a shocked voice. 'Why?'

Wendy stared down at her boots. She hated the idea of lying to him. Anyway, if she did, he'd see straight through it. 'Because Nanny hit Michael and she made John and me drink masses of castor oil.'

'Serves her right, then,' said Arthur Meredith with a

lightness that he didn't feel but that wafted the dreadful events straight out of Wendy's mind. He stood up. 'Now, run inside and find your Aunt Emily. I expect the wagonette's arrived by now and she'll be longing to see you.'

'Are we sleeping in the same room?' Wendy looked at the wild flowers in her hand. She'd forgotten to give them to him. Now they'd gone floppy.

'If you can fit into your bed.'

'I haven't grown *that* much, Uncle.' She handed him the flowers and ran into the house.

You're wrong about that, Wendy, he thought. He stared at the wilted cornflowers. Then he took them into the house and put them in water. Wild flowers always died so quickly. But it was the thought that counted and Wendy's thoughts were always precious to him.

'Wendy!' cried Liza. 'You're as black as a Green Park sheep!' She squeezed out the sponge in the soapy bathwater and rubbed it over Wendy's shoulders. 'What on earth have you been *doing*?'

'Helping Jock with Clover. She's Aunt Emily's mare.' Wendy sank into the warm water that filled the huge bath until only her face was above the surface. 'What do you think it's like to be a whale?'

'Couldn't say, I'm sure,' said Liza. 'Sit up now. Alice is here with your towel.'

'Lovely and warm from the fire.' Alice Jameson held out a thick white towel.

Wendy stepped onto the cork floor and let the hot towel enfold her. It was the most delicious feeling in the world.

'Will you read *The Secret Garden* to me, Wendy?' shouted Michael from the doorway.

For a moment, Wendy pretended her towel was a white evening gown and she was grown up and on her way out to dinner. 'Only if you stop shouting and get into bed, odious child!'

Liza laughed. 'I think Wendy could look after her brothers on her own!'

'But who would look after Wendy?' said Alice.

'I don't need anyone to look after me,' said Wendy in a voice that sounded fiercer than she meant it to. 'I can look after myself now.'

'Why don't Uncle Arthur and Aunt Emily have children?' asked John when they were all in bed and Liza had put out the light.

'Because they've got us, odious child,' said Michael.

'Don't call me "odious child",' said John crossly. 'You don't even know what it means.'

'Yes, I do! It means you smell.'

'That's odorous, silly,' said Wendy.

'Nobody's listening to me,' said John crossly. 'I said, why don't Uncle Arthur and Aunt Emily have children?'

Wendy thought of the photograph of Aunt

Emily's family on her writing desk. Her mother was Spanish, with a wide face and hair as thick as a horse's tail drawn back in a bun. Her father was a giant with wavy white hair and a beard. They sat in the middle of the picture with their eleven children arranged by height on either side of them, the tallest standing on the outside. Aunt Emily was the youngest, so she sat in the middle. All her brothers and sisters had children of their own, because Aunt Emily often talked about her other nephews and nieces. On Uncle Arthur's writing desk there was a picture of him and her mother when they were children.

'I'm not sure,' said Wendy slowly. 'I think it's something to do with litters like animals. Some have lots of babies and some don't have any.'

Nana turned around in her basket and grunted.

'Sorry, Nana, I wasn't talking about you,' said Wendy. 'You're not an animal.'

'What is she?' asked John sarcastically. 'A human disguised as a dog.'

Something like that.

'Maybe Aunt Emily only had one egg and it smashed,' said Michael suddenly.

'Rot,' said John.

'Not *rot*,' protested Michael. 'It's like those big white birds Wendy was telling me about.'

'You mean albatrosses?' said Wendy.

'That's them,' said Michael. 'Remember you said they made their nests on cliffs and laid only one egg.'

'Yes.'

'And sometimes the egg rolled off the cliff.'

'That's right.'

'Aunt Emily isn't a big white bird,' said John.

Michael sat up in bed. 'Aunt Emily's egg rolled off the dining-room table and she was so sad she didn't lay any more.'

'Don't be daft,' said John. 'Babies don't come from eggs. Storks bring them. Nanny showed us a picture, remember?'

Michael did remember the picture. 'Well, maybe the stork dropped Aunt Emily's baby,' he said. He huddled down in his bed. 'But at least they've got us, so they're not lonely.'

Wendy lay in bed half listening to her brothers' mad bickering. She was just old enough to remember a doctor bringing Michael to her mother in his black bag. And then Father had come out of the bedroom and announced to everyone that a baby boy had been born. It was all very confusing. She slipped into a dream and saw a gigantic stork carrying a doctor in his beak. And in the doctor's arms was a shiny white egg. 'I'll have an egg for breakfast,' said Mrs Darling, sitting in bed. And she was just about to crack the shell when Wendy rushed across the room and grabbed it out of her hand, because she knew there was a baby inside and the spoon would have bashed in its head. Then, in her dream, Nana took her hand and led her away.

Stop worrying about things you don't understand.

Wendy fell into a peaceful sleep.

8

It was a dangerous journey through the wild woods from Dry Gulch Beach and past the Rose River Rapids. Especially when you were carrying a picnic basket full of cherries. Already she had dodged a hungry grizzly bear and just missed being strangled by a python. As it was, the snake had eaten her straw hat, which was why she wasn't wearing it any more.

As Wendy picked her way down the track, a picture of the Crockers' cottage grew sharper and sharper in her mind. It was made of stone, with a slate-tiled roof and a front door that opened straight into a kitchen. Behind the kitchen was a tiny parlour and upstairs there were two bedrooms and a small attic where Thomas slept. It was exactly like lots of other cottages on the Rosegrove estate, but it was different too.

Very different.

Along the path to the front door were sculptures made of rotten tree stumps. Some were big, with painted faces and leaves for hair. Others were strange beasts crouched on the ground with sticks growing out of their backs like lizard spikes. Thomas had made them to guard the cottage. Every day he went into the woods to collect leaves and sticks to replace the ones that blew away or fell off in the night. But would they still be there? Wendy's mind went back to her dream in the train. Even as she thought about it, her mouth went dry. Would Thomas be the same? Or would he look at her and turn away because she was nothing but a little girl who once used to read to him when he was younger?

A plume of smoke drifted in the air. Through the trees Wendy saw the glint of the Crockers' stone cottage. Again she felt so nervous, she stopped.

Don't be so stupid, she told herself. *Of course he wants to see you. Peggy said so, didn't she?*

Already that morning Wendy had seen Peggy in the woods. She and John had been catching sticklebacks to put in the aquarium they were making. 'Thomas has been asking for you for months,' Peggy said. 'You must go and see him.'

Wendy heard herself ask. 'Are you sure?'

'Of course I'm sure.'

'What if he's too grown up now?'

And Peggy had rolled her eyes. 'Thomas is never going to grow up, you know that.'

Annie Crocker carefully put the last of the eggs she had collected that morning into the cabbage bag and lowered them into a pot of boiling water. She began to count to twenty, saying chimpanzee between each number. Peggy had told her it was the only way to count seconds. The things girls learned at school these days! At that moment, Wendy knocked on the door.

'Miss Wendy!' Annie Crocker wiped her hands on her long white apron and strode across the flagstones. 'I *am* pleased to see you!'

Wendy put down her basket and looked around her. Nothing had changed. Blue and white curtains still hung at the window. The kitchen table was still scrubbed as smooth as a butcher's block. Wendy recognised the heavy wooden box Mr Crocker had made for storing preserved eggs on the counter by the range. Twenty painted Rhode Island Reds danced across the lid. Twenty hens for twenty seconds. She remembered the day Thomas had painted them. 'Can I grease the eggs when they've cooled?'

'Goodness me, I almost forgot them!' Mrs Crocker pulled up the cabbage bag and plunged it into a sink of cold water. 'Of course you can. But you haven't come all this way to help me grease eggs, have you?'

Wendy felt her cheeks go pink. 'How is Thomas?' she asked quickly.

'Asking for you every day, of course. But tell me quickly about your mother. I've been expecting her for the past month or more.' She laid the cabbage bag on the table and carefully spread out the eggs. 'She'll be needing new petticoats for the winter.'

'Mother's in London,' said Wendy. Then she stopped. Mrs Crocker made a set of petticoats for her mother every year, but the strange thing was that Wendy knew her mother never wore them. Last winter's ones were still wrapped in brown paper and sitting at the bottom of the linen cupboard in London. When nobody was watching, Wendy often opened them up and buried her nose in the soft folds of wool. Mrs Crocker always put lavender between each petticoat. The smell took Wendy straight back to hot summer days and the strange beasts in the garden, and most of all, Thomas.

'Will she be coming down soon?'

Wendy saw her mother standing by her bedroom

window and staring down at the street with tears in her eyes. It seemed like a long time ago, yet it was only three days since she had said goodbye. Now, as she stood in the kitchen, she wished Mrs Crocker would stop asking about her mother. She wanted to forget London and the dark things she could not do anything about. 'I'm sorry, Mrs Crocker. I don't know. She said she had to talk about things with Father or something.'

Mrs Crocker heard a thin and almost hard sound in Wendy's voice. 'Well, then, there it is,' she said. She nodded towards the parlour. 'Now, off you go and give Thomas a lovely surprise.'

Thomas was sitting at his easel with his back to the parlour door. In front of him a window looked out over the tiny back garden. He was painting so intently that he didn't hear Wendy come into the room. This was the moment she had been dreaming about for months. She saw immediately that he had grown. Now he was as big as any of the young men who helped her uncle on the farm. She let her eyes wander about the room, to give her time to get used to this new Thomas. Two half-padded chairs sat on either side of the coal fire. A standard lamp with a pink frilly shade stood in the corner beside a rough wooden table. The floor was still covered with an old Turkish carpet from the nursery in Rosegrove. Her mother had asked Uncle Arthur if Thomas could have it so he could look at the patterns.

Wendy wanted to let Thomas know that she was in the room. But the longer she stood silent, the more difficult it was. Suddenly he went down on his knees in front of the canvas and began to scrape feverishly at the paint with a knife.

Up until now Wendy had not been able to see what he was painting. Now her hand flew to her mouth. The painting was the most horrible thing she had ever seen. It looked like boot blacking and blood and rabbits' innards, all smeared together. But it wasn't only the colours that were horrible. There was something about the shapes that made you feel sick and confused. It was as if the painting was laughing and screaming at you at the same time.

She watched as Thomas scooped up a gob of black paint and smeared a jagged line across the canvas. Then, to her horror, he began to rock from side to side and groan.

Wendy couldn't take her eyes away from the dreadful shapes. They were dragging her back to the night she had seen her father kissing Lady Cunningham and into her deepest, darkest nightmares. Her mind froze. It was the last thing she had expected to happen.

At that moment, Thomas turned. Wendy didn't know whether to run towards him or run away. His black hair flopped over a face that was sharper and dark. It was almost a man's face. They stared at each other for what seemed like ages but was no more than a couple of seconds.

'Wendy. Wendy. Wendy. Wendy.' Suddenly he smiled his brilliant smile.

Wendy couldn't help herself. She cried out with relief.

'I have waited every day for you!' He jumped up from his chair and stood towering over her, but now she didn't care.

'I've waited too.' There was something about his eyes. They shone like two black lights that could swallow you up. 'I've counted the days all summer.'

'I have waited every day.' He dragged his hands through her hair. 'Every day. Every day.' He turned and glared at the painting. 'Now there is this.'

Wendy forced herself to look at the painting. 'Yes.'

'I hate you,' said Thomas.

Wendy's heart battered at her ribs. Then she realised that he was talking not to her but to the painting. His hands fluttered at his sides like wild birds in a cage.

Wendy had never seen Thomas like this and for a moment she had no idea what to do. Why hadn't Peggy warned her about the painting? But perhaps Peggy didn't know. Thomas lunged at the canvas, growing more angry and agitated. Then Wendy had an inspiration. If Thomas talked to the painting, she would do the same thing.

'We don't want you here,' she said loudly. She turned the easel around, so the painting faced the wall.

For a moment, Thomas said nothing. Then he burst out laughing and clapped his hands. 'Read to me,' he ordered. He sat down at the table as usual and pulled out his sketchpad. 'Read to me, Wendy.'

Wendy pulled up her chair and sat down beside him. It was what they always did. The painting was forgotten. 'Aeroplanes,' announced Wendy, and opened a copy of the *Illustrated London News*. 'They are big wooden birds that carry men into the sky.'

* * *

But Thomas didn't forget the painting. While he was drawing, he kept turning around and glaring at it. Then suddenly he jumped up and manhandled the easel across the room and right in front of where Wendy was sitting. 'Burn it!' he yelled.

'Thomas! What's wrong?' Wendy looked at the painting, then up at his red, angry face. For the first time ever she was aware of how strong he was and she began to feel frightened. 'We don't want you!' she shouted at the painting again, hoping he would put it away.

'Hurts!' shouted Thomas. He raked his hand over the painting until his fingers were covered in red paint. 'I wait here! I wait here! *Hurts!*'

'I don't know what you're talking about,' said Wendy as calmly as she could, 'but I'm sorry you had to wait. I had to wait too. I wanted to see you, but I had to stay in London.' She held out her hand. 'Please, Thomas. Come and sit down again.'

But Thomas didn't move. 'I wait here. It hurts.' He pulled his finger over his white shirt, crossing his chest over and over with red lines. 'Sad. Sad. Sad. Sad.'

The door opened and Mrs Crocker came into the room. She looked at Wendy, then she looked at Thomas. 'What's the matter, Thomas? Why are you sad?'

Thomas yelled at the painting. 'I hate you! Burn!'

'Of course I'll burn it,' replied Mrs Crocker lightly. 'I've never wanted to burn anything so much in my life.' She turned to Wendy. 'You wouldn't believe it, dear, but that horrid thing has been stinking up the house for weeks now, but he wouldn't be parted with it. I'm so glad you're here.'

Thomas had become completely calm. Even as Mrs Crocker was speaking, he sat down at the table and began to draw so intently it was as if no one else was in the room.

Mrs Crocker picked up the painting and held it at

arm's length, as if it was a piece of rotten meat. Thomas didn't even look up.

'Why would he paint something so horrible?' whispered Wendy.

Mrs Crocker shook her head. 'He misses you and your mother terribly. A couple of weeks ago, he seemed to give up hope and started painting this thing.'

Wendy looked puzzled. 'Does Mother visit Thomas often?'

'From time to time and when she comes for a fitting. Sometimes she sings to him. He loves it when she sings to him. I expect your mother never thought to tell you.' Mrs Crocker took the red painting and walked into the kitchen. Wendy heard the clank of the stove door.

She crossed the parlour to where Thomas was hunched over his pad. 'Aeroplane,' he said proudly. Wendy looked at his picture. It was Rosegrove from the sky. In the garden, Uncle Arthur and Aunt Emily sat beside each other at a table. Across the lawn and over the paddock, she could see the Rose River Rapids shining like a silver ribbon through the dark leaves of the trees. She saw herself and John and Peggy fishing from the river bank. And at the end of a track she saw the Crockers' cottage with the huge oak in the garden. A figure in a floating dress was flying over the tree and down towards the cottage. At first Wendy thought Thomas had painted a fairy, but the figure was as big as any of the others in the picture.

'Angel,' crooned Thomas. 'Angel. Angel.' He stroked the little figure and rocked from side to side. Long hair flew from the figure's heart-shaped face. It had a fine tilted-up nose and a smile played on its lips. Wendy knew the face because she had seen it since she was a baby.

The angel was her mother.

9

Two weeks later Wendy was building a den in Cobra Clearing in the middle of Wolverine Woods with Peggy and John. She had spent almost every afternoon with Thomas, reading and watching him draw, until yesterday Mrs Crocker had taken her aside. *Don't get me wrong, Miss Wendy, but you won't be here for ever and Thomas needs to get used to that. And Peggy's hardly seen you.* At first Wendy was upset, but then she realised that Mrs Crocker was right. She was thinking of herself and not Thomas, and it was true that she had spent hardly any time with John and Peggy. Now it was the beginning of September. Soon they would be going back to London.

'I *still* don't understand,' said Peggy Crocker as she dragged a pine branch over the ground. 'If you hated your nanny so much, why didn't you run away?' Peggy was fascinated by John and Wendy's London life and she never tired of talking about it. She carefully fitted the pine branch onto the enormous pile of branches. 'If I had someone like that looking after me, I'd hide in the woods and make sure no one could find me.'

Wendy laughed. 'There aren't any woods in London. Only some big bushes in Hyde Park and there are so many people, someone would find you right away. Thing is, Peggy, it's different in London, you can't go anywhere on your own.'

'Not even to the pond?'

Wendy shook her head. 'There are too many streets to cross.'

'So what? I walk three miles to school every morning.' Peggy pulled a face. 'And there are lots of *crossroads*.'

'It's not how far. It's all the motor cars and buses and cabs. People get knocked down every day.'

'A motor car killed the milkman's horse last

month,' said Peggy, determined not be outdone. 'Smashed his wagon to bits.' She poked the ground with a stick. Even though London sounded dirty and crowded, she read every magazine Wendy brought down and sometimes cut out particular photographs and stuck them in her scrap-book under the heading 'Things I Want to See'.

'I *hate* motor cars,' said Wendy suddenly.

'But I thought your father had one.'

'He does, but none of us likes it.'

Peggy remembered a photograph she had seen of a woman just like Mrs Darling wearing a huge motoring coat covered in braid and tassels. It was like the sort of cloak a princess would wear in the faraway Eastern lands. In Peggy's head, motoring was all bound up with Aladdin and Sinbad and the Arabian Nights. 'Your mother must like it.'

'She hates it most of all.'

Wendy had not thought of her mother for ages. It

wasn't that difficult, as Mrs Darling had never arrived, which in one way was sad, because she and Uncle Arthur and Aunt Emily liked each other so much. But in another, everything seemed so much simpler without her. Liza and Alice never made a fuss about anything and everyone got on with their lives, just as they always did at Rosegrove.

'I thought all ladies loved motor cars,' said Peggy. 'John said Lady Cunningham adored them.'

'John's got no right to talk about the Cunninghams!' snapped Wendy.

Peggy looked puzzled. 'Why not? All he said was that Sir Alfred refused to buy one and Henry was nasty and Letitia was silly.' She dropped her stick and sat down on the ground beside Wendy. 'Is something wrong?'

Wendy ripped up a handful of grass and let it fall from her fingers. 'I don't like Lady Cunningham and thinking about Henry and Letitia reminds me we have to go back to London soon, and I hate it.'

'Then why play with them?' Peggy shook her head. 'It seems crazy to me.'

'It *is* crazy,' said Wendy. 'Because I'm sure they don't like us either. But mother says we have to.'

Peggy shook her head. The more she heard about John and Wendy's life in London, the odder it sounded. 'Come on,' she said at last. 'Let's finish the den.'

'Sorry, Peggy. I didn't mean to be cross.' Wendy rubbed her hands over her face. 'But you don't have to live in London.'

'Then live in the den! We'll pretend it's your country house,' cried Peggy. 'It's almost ready anyway.' She pulled across the branch door and they crawled inside. 'Come on! Let's test it out.'

Wendy lay on the old blanket she'd taken from the box in the nursery and stared up at a domed ceiling of branches propped up in a circle and tied together with string. It was green and murky and completely wonderful.

'I could hide here for ever,' she said dreamily. 'No one would find me.'

A branch was dragged back. John stood in the sunshine and peered in. 'Mother's coming,' he said.

Wendy sat up. 'How do you know?'

'Uncle Arthur told me,' said John. 'Jock's getting her from the station. She'll be here by now.' He sat down cross-legged and stared at Wendy. 'You don't think she's come to take us back, do you?'

Wendy chewed her lips. 'That was what she said she might do.'

'When?' asked John fiercely.

'When you were waiting for the bus and I was in her room.'

'That's it, then.'

'Maybe not,' said Peggy. 'Maybe she's bringing Charlie Pickles to meet your uncle.'

'Charlie Pickles?' cried John. He turned to Wendy

and they both stared at Peggy. 'Why would she do that?'

'I thought you knew,' said Peggy uncomfortably.

'Knew what?' asked Wendy. 'Nobody tells us anything.'

Peggy stared at the coarse green blanket. 'Charlie Pickles is coming to Rosegrove to be my father's apprentice. There isn't another carpenter on the estate and your mother thought –'

'Our mother!' cried Wendy. 'Oh, no!' She turned to John and knew he was thinking the same as she was.

'I don't understand,' said Peggy.

'Of course you don't understand,' said Wendy. 'Why should you understand? The point is, now Liza will stay at Rosegrove and marry Charlie Pickles, and if Liza can't look after us we'll have to have some horrible new nanny.'

'Why can't you look after yourselves?'

'Because we're not *allowed* to,' yelled Wendy. 'I've

told you again and again. We're not allowed to do anything on our own. They even ask if we've been to the lavatory every morning.'

'That's disgusting,' said Peggy. 'Tell them it's none of their business.'

'You try it,' said Wendy. She put on Nanny Holborn's voice. 'A dose of castor oil will sort you out proper.'

'Then tell her you want to stay,' said Peggy.

'We can't tell our mother anything,' said Wendy. 'She doesn't listen.'

'Why not try?'

'No point.' Wendy pulled back the branch. 'I'm going to see Thomas.'

'Don't say goodbye to him,' said Peggy suddenly.

'I wasn't going to. Anyway, why not? I'll have to sooner or later.'

'He doesn't understand when people say goodbye,'

said Peggy. 'He thinks he'll never see them again. Last Christmas he was in such a state, we had to call the doctor.' She swallowed. 'It's better not to say anything.'

'Why didn't anyone tell me?' said Wendy.

'Mum told your mother,' said Peggy, looking at the ground. When she looked up, Wendy had gone.

As Wendy ran across the paddock her head pounded and her legs felt as if they belonged to someone else. Why hadn't her mother warned her? She would rather have died than upset Thomas. As she turned down the cart track to the Crockers' cottage, she realised that she was almost in tears, which would upset Thomas more than anything. *You're being silly,* she shouted at herself. *You don't even know if you're leaving.* But still she wanted to see him. She wanted to sit down and read to him. No, she was feeling too muddled for that. She would just look at him through the window and go home to tea.

She got down on her hands and knees and crept behind the stump that looked like a lizard, the one that was furthest from the house. Then she moved up to the hedge that ran along the garden. There was a gap in the hedge in front of the parlour window . . .

Above the trees the sky had turned dark purple and a hot sticky wind rattled the leaves. A thunderstorm was coming. She would have to hurry. She crawled as fast as she could over the grass behind the hedge. Mr Crocker's spaniel barked in the yard.

The gap was exactly where she remembered. Wendy settled herself on the grass. For a moment she didn't look up. She wanted to get her breath back and she wanted to do everything slowly, so that when she did peer through the gap she would remember everything she saw . . . She leaned forward and peered through the gap.

She froze.

Thomas and her mother stood wrapped in each

other's arms in the garden. Her mother's head was buried in Thomas's neck. Wendy watched Thomas draw his fingers through her mother's hair. She saw her mother pull him closer.

Wendy tried to look away, but found she could not. Her mother looked up. For a terrible moment she seemed to be staring straight at her. Her face had an expression that Wendy had never seen before. There was love and something else she couldn't understand.

An insect crawled over Wendy's fingers. She looked down and saw a beetle, rainbow colours glittering in its shiny black back. Normally she would have watched it, but now she shook it off. When she looked up, Thomas and her mother had gone.

Wendy fell back on the wet grass. Every part of her body ached as if she had been kicked. Now she understood why Thomas had stroked the little figure of her mother. He loved her and, when she didn't come to him, he painted the horrible painting that made him so unhappy. Wendy thought of the unopened brown-paper parcels in London. Now she knew why her mother ordered so many petticoats. It was the only way she could see Thomas without people asking questions.

Wendy rolled back and forth on the wet grass. Why did her mother have to steal Thomas for herself? How could she be so cruel? She thought about her father and Lady Cunningham. Was it possible that her mother had found out and was using Thomas to get back at him? Wendy held her head in her hands.

Thunder rumbled and rain splattered on the ground. She could feel the cold, heavy drops sinking through her hair to her scalp. The garden was empty. She tried to pretend that she had imagined it all. But she could see Thomas's fingers pulling at her mother's hair. Suddenly Letitia's laughter was all around her. She saw her smirking and rubbing two dolls together. *As long as no one finds out, she doesn't care . . .*

She stumbled along the hedge and past the oak lizard, then she ran as fast as she could along the track and into the woods. By now the rain was pouring down. Even though there was more shelter under the leaves, her clothes were soon soaked through to her skin. She stopped under a dripping chestnut tree and leaned her head against the trunk. She needed time to think. It was impossible to go all the way back to Rosegrove in this rain. And the prospect of seeing her mother was unbearable.

Then she remembered the den. Peggy was right. No one would find her there and they had made it as waterproof as possible. She turned and ran towards Cobra Clearing. She was almost there when she tripped over a tree root and fell face first onto the ground.

Wendy didn't know how long she had been lying in the rain. When she sat up one side of her forehead throbbed painfully. She reached up to feel the place that hurt and found that it was sticky and wet. She wiped it with the edge of her pinafore and discovered her head was covered in blood. Rain and blood dripped from her forehead into her eye and down the front of her pinafore. Ahead she could just make out the mound of leafy branches. She didn't dare stand up. So she crawled over the muddy grass until she reached the den. Then she pulled back the door and crept inside.

Wendy lay on the old nursery blanket. She told Peggy that she had done a good job, which was true, because the den was really quite dry inside. Peggy didn't answer. Perhaps she was not even there. In a strange, dreamy way, Wendy was glad that her head hurt so much, because it meant she did not have to think about anything else, except falling forwards into a big, black pit.

10

Arthur Meredith watched his sister push a forkful of veal in celery sauce around her plate. So far she had barely eaten anything. She hadn't even noticed that Mrs Fielding had cooked all of her favourite dishes.

Across the table, Emily Meredith met her husband's eye. 'We were thinking you might like to take over part of the garden,' she said lightly. 'It would be something for you to do while you're here, and Coleridge will give you any help that's needed.' Emily smiled. 'Would you like that?'

Mrs Darling looked up. For weeks now, everything she ate had tasted of iron filings. It was disgusting. After a while, she had realised that the only solution was to give up eating. Anyway, George was never in the house at meal times these days, so it was a good opportunity to economise on food bills.

Emily leaned forward. 'Are you quite well, dear?'

Mrs Darling tried to focus on the face in front of her. She liked her sister-in-law. It was such a pity the poor dear couldn't have children. She'd heard there was a new doctor in London who'd had great success with childless couples. Something to do with mustard powder.

'I do beg your pardon, Emily, I was miles away. What did you say?'

'We thought you might like to redesign part of the garden,' said Arthur Meredith slowly.

'Why would I want to do that?' Mrs Darling laughed. 'I have so many things to do as it is and I don't get around to any of them.' She frowned as if she was trying to remember something. 'Are the children well? I haven't seen them yet.'

'They're all *very* well,' said Emily warmly. 'And Liza and Alice have been marvellous.'

'Wendy has grown up so much,' added Arthur. He

smiled. 'She's turned into quite a serious thinker these days.'

'Wendy will always make a mountain out of a molehill,' replied Mrs Darling. She looked down at her uneaten food. For some reason it reminded her of Nanny Holborn's obsession with clean plates. 'We had to get rid of Nanny Holborn, you know.'

'Wendy told me.' Arthur Meredith gave his sister a puzzled look. She really seemed to be in a most peculiar state. But he knew his sister well enough not to press her. If he asked her a direct question, she would only make things up. Sooner or later, the truth would come out.

'What exactly did Wendy say?' Mrs Darling smiled a bright, artificial smile that was quite unlike her.

Arthur Meredith found it impossible to read the smile. Was she angry with her daughter? There had been no need to accuse her of making mountains out of molehills. Or was she embarrassed that Wendy might have broken some peculiar rule in George Darling's household and told him the truth? Well, Darling was a fool and Arthur didn't want to get Wendy into any trouble with her mother. 'She mentioned that Nanny Holborn had gone, that was all.'

'I'm surprised she didn't say more,' said Mrs Darling wearily. 'The woman was a wretched mistake. The truth is, George dismissed her. He said we couldn't afford her wages.'

There was a *clink* as Emily reached awkwardly for her glass. She looked between her husband and her sister-in-law. 'I must just go and see how Mrs Fielding is doing with the lobster. It would be such a shame to overcook it.'

'Don't bother for me,' said Mrs Darling in a gay, brittle voice. 'Anyway, it's all too boring and there's nothing much to say. George is broke and behaving monstrously.' She picked up her glass. But her hand trembled so much that she had to put it down again.

Arthur Meredith reached over and took his sister's hand. 'If there is anything we can do –'

Mrs Darling shook her head. 'You've done enough

for me already.' Rain hammered at the window and there was a loud crack of lightning. She put her hand on her brother's arm. 'I'm just glad to be here, safe.'

Someone knocked violently on the door and it flew open. Liza came into the room. John was with her, dressed in his pyjamas with a raincoat over the top.

'Something terrible's happened, ma'am,' cried Liza.

'Wendy's missing,' shouted John, 'We've looked for her everywhere.'

'What do you mean, *missing*?' cried Mrs Darling. 'Surely she came home for tea?'

'We thought she did, ma'am,' stammered Liza. 'At least, I thought Alice knew where she was. And Alice thought I knew where she was because Nana was in the nursery. But . . . oh dear, ma'am!' cried Liza, putting her face into her hands.

'Have you looked in the stables?' said Emily Meredith. 'She's been helping Jock with Clover's new foal.'

'We looked there first,' said Liza. 'And in the gardens and the vegetable store, because she's been sorting out last year's apples for Mrs Fielding, but, oh dear . . . Tell your uncle what you told me, Master John.'

'We built a den in Cobra Clearing,' said John.

'*Where?*' said Arthur Meredith.

'It's in Wolverine Woods.' John grabbed his uncle by the hand. 'Come on. I'll show you!'

Wendy sat at the end of a table covered in so many candles and so much silver and glass that it hurt her eyes. The walls were smeared with gobs of black and red paint. Her chair was so high that her feet dangled in the air. If she looked down she felt so dizzy she was afraid she would fall and break her neck on the floor. In front of her was a silver plate full of wriggling sticklebacks.

'Don't you like sticklebacks?' said Letitia at her side. 'John caught them.'

'They are supposed to be in an aquarium,' explained Wendy. 'Not on a plate.'

'Eat them,' commanded Letitia.

Wendy picked up her knife and fork. 'But they're still alive.'

'Eat them *up*,' yelled Letitia.

'It's terribly rude to scrape a silver plate,' snapped Lady Cunningham on her other side. 'You ought to know better.'

Wendy pressed down her knife as gently as she could. Silver shrieked against silver.

'Have you nothing to say for yourself?' cried Lady Cunningham. 'I do so *hate* a hole in the conversation.' She glared at Wendy from underneath a spray of black ostrich feathers.

Wendy opened her mouth to speak, but nothing came out.

'Gracious, child. Have you been struck dumb?'

Lady Cunningham laughed, and Wendy noticed her teeth were made out of pointed chandelier crystals.

'Wendy is the most boring person I know,' said Letitia. Her eyes were outlined in black and she had painted her lips red. 'She thinks she knows everything, but she's really stupid.'

Lady Cunningham laughed and a hundred tiny candles sparkled in her mouth. 'Oh dear! How dull! Then we shall have to amuse ourselves.'

She clapped her hands.

The door opened and a man in a magician's suit pushed a puppet theatre into the room. A red velvet curtain hung down in front of the stage.

'Let the show begin,' cried Lady Cunningham.

The curtains swung back. Thomas was standing in the garden. Her mother was walking towards him.

'No! Thomas! No!' Wendy screamed.

Somewhere Lady Cunningham laughed and

somewhere something cold was pressed onto her forehead. She looked up. Now she was lying down, but everything around her was black.

'Poor child,' said Alice. 'She's calling for Thomas.'

'She's feverish,' said Liza. Her voice cracked. 'If only her mother would leave Thomas be!'

Wendy felt a hand smoothing back her hair. 'Annie Crocker said she was there this afternoon. Even before she came up to the house.'

'She should give him up,' said Alice. 'He'll ruin her life.'

'Perhaps he already has.'

'Why doesn't anyone care about me?' screamed Wendy, but no sound came out. She tried to sit up so they would listen, but she couldn't move.

'The child's quite mad,' cried Lady Cunningham.

'Wriggling about like a worm! Do you know what we do to mad people, Letitia?' She howled with laughter. Then she sank her sharp crystal teeth into Wendy's head.

Wendy sat up in bed and screamed.

'Lawks-a-mercy!' cried Liza. 'Quick, Alice! Fetch the doctor!'

Someone's crying, thought Wendy.

She opened her eyes. She saw her mother hunched in a chair beside her. Crying. For a moment, she could not think where she was, or how she had got there. Then it came back to her and she closed her eyes and pretended she was still asleep. She didn't want her mother to know she was awake. She didn't want to have to look into her face. She didn't want to see her mother ever again.

Wendy let her thoughts wobble about in her mind. Is this what hating someone feels like? You hear them crying and you pretend you're asleep. Perhaps you're even glad to hear them crying. Well, she wasn't glad to hear her mother crying. She just wanted her to go away, because it was all too tiring to listen to.

She drifted back to sleep.

Maybe I should ask her to go away, thought Wendy, the next time she woke up and her mother was still there. All of this crying, it's as if I've done something wrong to her but it's the other way round. I heard what Alice said to Liza. *She should give him up.* She's right. Why should she ruin his life? Wendy frowned. No, it wasn't that. It was the other way round. *He'll ruin her life.*

Stop crying! she wanted to shout at her mother. What difference was it going to make now? But each time she heard her mother's sobs, she knew there was something she had forgotten . . . but she was too tired to remember what it was. She drifted back to sleep again.

One day, Wendy felt her mother's fingers smooth

back her hair. *Don't touch me!* she wanted to scream. *Leave me alone!* But the fingers didn't go away. They ran through her hair and cupped her head gently. Despite herself, Wendy felt comforted, and a picture formed in her mind. She was peering through the hedge into the Crockers' garden. Thomas was stroking her mother's hair. Her mother was pulling Thomas towards her. Her mother looked straight at her. Then Wendy remembered what she had forgotten.

Her mother was crying.

Wendy groaned and turned over in her bed. How could her mother love Thomas and be sad? Could it be that she felt guilty about what she was doing? Her father didn't cry when he kissed Lady Cunningham. But her father never felt guilty about anything, because he thought only of himself. Tears ran onto her pillowcase.

'Wendy, Wendy.' Her mother's fingers touched her wet cheeks. 'Please. Open your eyes. Let me talk to you.'

But Wendy was afraid to open her eyes. She didn't know if she would ever be able to look into her mother's face without seeing her with Thomas. It was one thing to remember it in her head, but to see it for real was unbearable. 'I hate you,' she muttered into her pillow. 'Leave me alone.' She turned her head away.

Later Nana got up from her basket in the corner. She padded across the room and licked the arm that dangled from the bed.

'I don't understand, Nana. I don't understand.'

No one understands love.

'Sit up, Wendy,' said Liza. 'The doctor says you're to drink orange juice every morning.' She clanked the breakfast tray down on the bedside table and plumped up the pillows. 'Then you won't be so tired all the time.'

For two weeks Wendy had stayed in bed, refusing to talk to anyone. Not even Nana. If people came to see her, she said she was too tired for company. All she wanted to do was read her books and be left alone.

'Wendy isn't tired,' said Michael, standing with John in the doorway. 'She's sad.'

Wendy sat up. Why couldn't Michael keep his mouth shut?

'I'm not sad,' said Wendy. She pulled a crazy face. 'I'm mad. Part of my brain fell out when I hit my head.'

'Wendy!' cried Liza in a flustered voice. 'You can't be all that ill if you can say horrible things like that.'

'It's the sort of thing mad people say.' Wendy picked up her glass from the breakfast tray and drank it down in one gulp. It was almost worth being in bed if you got fresh orange juice every morning. 'And I don't want anyone feeling sorry for me either.'

'Who said I was sorry for you?' asked John. 'You probably *are* mad.'

'If I'm mad, you're stupid.'

'Stop bickering,' said Liza. But instead of straightening the bed, she opened the chest of drawers and began to put out Wendy's clothes.

'What are you doing?'

'What I should have done days ago,' said Liza. 'John, run and tell your mother Wendy is getting up today.'

But John stood by the door and didn't move. 'Are you going to marry Charlie Pickles? Peggy says it's like he's been living here all his life. She says it's only a matter of time.'

'Does she now,' said Liza crossly. 'Well, you tell Peggy Crocker from me to keep her nose out of my affairs.'

'So it's true,' said Wendy. 'You *are* going to marry Charlie Pickles.' She fell back on her pillows. 'And we get a new nanny foisted on us.'

'I don't want a new nanny!' wailed Michael.

'Look here,' said Liza sternly. 'I will not marry

Charlie Pickles until I'm good and ready. And right now I've got other things to do.'

'Like what?' asked John suspiciously.

'Like look after you lot. Now go and find your mother. She's been worried sick. And as for you, Wendy, *get up!*'

It was a black and white photograph but George Darling saw it in living colour. Mrs Darling was seated, in a yellow satin dress with a fitted bodice draped with lace. Her long skirt hung in wide glossy folds to the carpet. Wendy stood in white slippers on her mother's right hand side. She held a doll in her hand and her blonde hair was tied back with a ribbon. She was only four but she looked pleased, as if she knew she was part of something important. John sat on his mother's left. He had a puzzled expression on his face and was bolt upright, as if he didn't like the feel of the frilly white gown he had to wear.

Mrs Darling was smiling down at John. The fine curve of her cheekbone and full lines of her mouth made her look particularly beautiful. A single pearl pendant lay on her bosom.

George Darling swallowed a gulp of whisky.

Something had gone wrong and he didn't know how it had happened. His wife was no longer the woman in the photograph. She was a big-eyed phantom gliding through the house, never speaking. George Darling looked at Wendy standing so proudly beside her mother. There was something wrong with her too and it had been going on for months. Every time he came near her, she shrank away as if he had leprosy. He banged the photograph back onto the piano. And now she'd fallen over and hit her head, and everyone was behaving as if the Anarchists had killed the king.

He poured another slug of whisky. The stopper of the decanter made a *clang* in the silent house. What was a man supposed to do when his wife left him alone in London? No wonder he looked for company elsewhere. Especially now that the Cunninghams had returned from Northumberland.

George Darling thought back to the previous evening. Lady Sheffield had obligingly placed him next to

Lady Cunningham at the table and they had talked about motor cars almost all the way through dinner. He had barely exchanged a word with Mrs Benting on his right. But then Mrs Benting had a face like wizened parsnip and her frizzy hair stank of stale powder. Sir Alfred, on her other side, had had to do most of the talking. It hadn't pleased him. But George Darling did not care whether he was pleased or not.

Silly old buffer, Sir Alfred. Said he didn't approve of motor cars. What was the point of taking a stand against the combustion engine? It was progress and nothing was going to stop it. As he had said himself last night, if God meant horses to stay on the roads, he would have given them wheels. Rather witty, he had thought. But Sir Alfred had hardly acknowledged him and then started talking to Mrs Benting about some painter or other. A snub. A damned piece of rudeness. *Silly old buffer.*

George Darling clanged the decanter again and

poured what was left in it into his glass. 'I could have had any woman I wanted,' he muttered to himself. 'And I chose a fairy-tale princess who can't grow up.' Suddenly he was furious. 'You're all bloody useless!' he shouted at the photograph. Then he threw it on the floor and stamped on it, and rang the bell.

Down in the kitchen, Gorman, the footman, was having a cup of tea with Mrs Jenkins. They both heard the crash and the ringing of the bell.

Neither of them moved.

'He's smashing the photograph again,' said Gorman, looking up at the ceiling. 'I don't know how she puts up with him.'

Mrs Jenkins put a piece of shortbread in her mouth and wiped away the crumbs with a napkin. 'She doesn't know the half of it, poor lamb.'

They exchanged knowing looks.

'*Lady* Cunningham,' said Mrs Jenkins sarcastically.

'My friend Nellie's a parlour maid there. Her Ladyship's daddy made a mint out of selling bad beef to troops in the African war. *Tchaah!* Look at her!'

'Do you think he knows?'

'Sir Alfred?' said Mrs Jenkins. 'I should think not! Nellie says he'd divorce her if he ever found out, scandal or no scandal.'

The bell rang again, for longer this time.

Gorman stood up, yawning. 'I'd better go.'

'I don't suppose he's in for dinner?'

'Shall I ask him?'

Mrs Jenkins shrugged. 'He's only getting leftovers.'

Gorman found George Darling leaning on the sideboard. The decanter was empty. Gorman began to sweep up the glass.

'Never mind about that. Put out my motoring clothes!'

Gorman looked at his master's face. It was red and blotchy and his speech was slurred. 'Excuse the liberty, sir, but do you think that's wise?'

'Wise?' shouted George Darling at the two faces in front of him. 'Whaddayou know about what's wise?'

'Nothing, sir. I'll see to the clothes right away, sir.'

'About time too. Oh, and Gorman?'

The footman turned on his way out of the door. 'Yes, sir.'

'Somebody's stealing the whisky.'

Time to start looking for a new place, thought Gorman.

An hour later, George Darling sat behind the wheel of his yellow Lanchester and drove along Pall Mall towards the Strand. How dare that ludicrous footman suggest he was unwise to go motoring? Nothing like a spin to clear the head. Besides, he knew the roads like the back of his hand.

He'd take a turn along the Embankment then back along Birdcage Walk past St James's. Might even stop in the park. He cut a fine figure in his tartan motoring coat with its horn buttons and high standing collar. Every time he stopped, the ladies clustered around the car like dainty moths around a flame. Hadn't he tipped his cap half a dozen times already?

As George Darling turned into the Strand, he became aware of a new noise above the clatter of the engine. At first he couldn't work out what it was. The noise of the motor's engine was like a lullaby to his ears and he was beginning to feel strangely sleepy. Suddenly there was a roar. A roar of voices. An enormous crowd of women turned a corner and began walking up the Strand. There must have been hundreds of them, and they were all waving tiny white banners and shouting, 'Right to Vote! Right to Vote!'

Behind him and around him motor cars, cabs and

omnibuses slowed right down. The air was filled with a different noise. Hundreds of women began to smash shop windows. From every part of the street, onlookers jumped and screamed as glass shattered at their feet. Terrified shop assistants ran onto the pavement. Policemen stormed into the crowd, waving their truncheons and pushing people out of their way. Some of them dragged screaming women to the side of the road. Small angry groups surrounded others and pinned them down, yelling for the police.

George Darling was maddened with rage. Bloody suffragettes with their lunatic ideas! How dare they damage property? How dare they risk the lives of decent hard-working people? He squeezed the car's horn and hollered at the top of his voice. The next thing he knew, he had driven into a flower seller's basket and crushed a fruit boy's barrow. Hundreds of apples rolled into the shattered glass. George turned the car hard left down the nearest side street. Something crunched in the gearbox and the car juddered to a halt. When he put his foot down on the accelerator again, he found himself going backwards and heading straight for the crowd.

All around him women were shouting, 'Fight for the Vote! Fight for the Vote!' The flower seller shook her ham-sized fist at him and bellowed for the police. The boy selling apples picked one up and threw it. The apple hit George Darling smack in the ear. He jumped out of his car, his head throbbing with pain. When he saw that he had dented the front wing and broken the headlamp, a crazy rage surged through his body. He would tell these bloody women what he thought of them if it was the last thing he did. He ran like a wild animal.

Esther Cunningham stood by a broken shop window, frightened and shaken. She watched in horror as George Darling tore bellowing into the crowd, then she stumbled over to the policeman who only a moment before had thrown her violently onto the side of the street.

Wendy

* * *

It was a beautiful day at Rosegrove. The sky was high and blue and there was a crispness in the air that promised autumn. Wendy stood in the vegetable garden with Nana. Mrs Fielding had asked her to pick the last of the tarragon and mint for drying, but so far she had only got as far as the pumpkin patch. She stood and stared at the huge leaves and prickly stalks that trailed over the ground like snakes.

'What do you think it's like to live in a pumpkin, Nana?'

Orange, you daft monkey.

She laughed. 'I thought you'd say that. Want to see me do a cartwheel?' She put down the two shallow wooden baskets Mrs Fielding had given her and did a spidery roll on the grass.

That was terrible.

Wendy burst out laughing and did it again.

Ten minutes later, the two trug baskets Mrs

Fielding had given her were filled to the top with tarragon and mint. She walked down the path and closed the painted white gate behind her.

'Sit down, my dear.'

Mrs Darling stared at her brother's face. 'Arthur! What's wrong? You look as white as a sheet.'

'I've got bad news, I'm afraid.' He took his sister by the arm and led her to a chair. 'Please sit down.'

'Is it George?'

Arthur nodded. 'There's been an incident involving his motor car.'

Mrs Darling buried her face in her hands. 'Oh, God! I knew this would happen. He drives like a lunatic.' She stood up and began to pace across the room. 'I won't go out with him any more. And I won't let him drive the children either.' Suddenly she realised that she hadn't asked whether he was hurt.

'He's not hurt,' said her brother, as if he was reading her mind. He held up a letter. 'This came today. It's from Sir Alfred Cunningham's daughter.'

'Esther?' cried Mrs Darling.

'There was a demonstration of suffragettes in the Strand last week. Some women threw stones. Some shop windows were broken.' He took a breath. 'Apparently George was passing in his car and, ah, lost his temper.'

'What did he do?' asked Mrs Darling in a voice that was barely above a whisper.

'He damaged property, insulted the police and swore at the demonstrators,' said her brother.

'Dear God,' said Mrs Darling. 'Was he drunk?'

'Yes.'

Through the open window, they could hear John and Wendy shouting happily in the garden.

Arthur Meredith had hoped that his sister's visit to Rosegrove would give her a chance to spend more time with her children, or at least to take an interest in the house or the garden. But as each day passed, she spent more time on her own. After Wendy's accident, she had sat with her for two nights running, but once the girl was out of danger she had just about ignored her. And the saddest thing was that the children seemed perfectly happy with the situation. Indeed, he was practically sure that Wendy was actually doing her best to avoid her mother.

'I still don't understand why Esther wrote,' said Mrs Darling. 'Why didn't George?'

Arthur sighed. 'He probably hoped you wouldn't find out because you're here. The point is that the police want to press a charge of damage to property and public affray, and Miss Cunningham is the chief witness. She wants you to know she does not intend to testify against him.' He handed her the letter. 'Read the letter yourself. She's included the press cutting.'

'It's in the papers?' cried Mrs Darling, aghast.

'I'm afraid so,' said her brother. 'But at least he's not mentioned by name.' He put his hand on her shoulder. 'I think you ought to go back to London immediately.'

Wendy pushed her feet as hard as she could and soared high into the air. If she opened her eyes quickly when the swing was at its very highest, she could pretend she was a bird flying over Rosegrove.

Out of the corner of her eye, she could see the glass hot-houses glittering in the sun beside the walled garden. She could see the forest of brick chimneys growing out of the roofs and the weathervane in the shape of a unicorn spinning around at the very top.

The swing sailed backwards past the row of yew trees that looked like peacocks and the crescent-shaped beds with their brilliant blue and yellow and orange flowers.

'Wendy! Wendy!'

She soared upwards again and saw John running towards her.

'Go away!' she shouted. 'I'm thinking!'

It was strange. Some days she felt better, others she felt dreadful again. Swinging made it easier to think. On her bad days, thinking about things that were horrible didn't hurt as much when she was swinging.

Like Thomas.

Every day since Wendy had got up from her bed, she'd gone straight to the swing and thought of Thomas. And after she had swung back and forth for a long time, she could say to herself, *I'll never see Thomas again.* And the more she said it, the easier it was to believe. Especially if you pretended you were a bird and could fly away any time you wanted.

'W-e-n-d-y!' John stood below her and bellowed as loudly as he could.

Wendy dragged her sandals on the ground. The swing juddered to a stop.

'What?' Then she saw John's face was bright red and he was chewing his lips as if they were covered in bits of dry glue. 'We're going home, aren't we?'

'Tomorrow.'

'Go away,' said Wendy harshly. 'I want to swing.'

'All you think about is yourself,' shouted John.

But Wendy leaned back and shoved herself forward. She had to get back up in the air before the lump in her throat turned into tears.

12

Gorman had to wrinkle his nose as he walked into George Darling's study. The master had hardly left it for a week and it stank of whisky and stale cigars. Two plates of curling sandwiches lay untouched on the sideboard. 'Excuse me, sir,' he said. 'Mrs Darling and the children have arrived.'

Mr Darling jumped up from his desk as if he'd been stung by a bee. 'I beg your pardon?'

'She's back from Rosegrove, sir, I believe.'

'What on earth for?'

'No idea, sir.'

George Darling dragged his fingers through his hair and his eye strayed across to the decanter on the sideboard. 'I'll speak to her presently.'

As soon as the footman closed the door, he poured himself a large whisky. 'Now what am I going to do?' he muttered to himself. He gulped at his drink and went back to his desk, not because he had any business there, but because it was where he'd spent so many hours lately and he could not imagine sitting anywhere else.

The telegram was still open. He'd read it so many times now he knew it off by heart.

The Directors of Swan Marshall & Partners regret to inform you that after recent newspaper accounts of an incident in which they understand you were concerned they no longer require your services Stop Please return any business correspondence concerning this office as soon as possible Stop

He swallowed the last of the whisky. The books and paintings on the wall looked soft-edged and blurred, as if they belonged in a dream. He grabbed the telegram on his desk and shouted at it. 'Bloody fools! You'll be finished without me. No one else has my touch!' He knew exactly who had told them. It was that weasel of a clerk, Higgins, who was obsessed with motor cars. He was the only one who would have recognised the Lanchester.

A servant's bell rang and he remembered his wife was upstairs. 'D'you think she knows?' he asked himself out loud. 'Happened ages ago now.' The thought of having to explain everything to his wife, the humiliation, damn it, the *consequences,* made his insides turn to water. He crumpled up the telegram and threw it into the waste-paper basket. Then he put on his hat and coat and walked out into the street.

Mrs Darling stood at her bedroom window, untying her coat and looking out at the trees in the square. Soon summer would be over and all those glossy green leaves would turn red and yellow and drop to the ground. She found herself wondering if she would still be standing at the same window when autumn came. And she discovered she didn't care.

All the way up on the train, she had tried to rehearse what to say to George. He would know as well as she did that a charge of public affray and damage to public property would cause a frightful scandal. And coming just now, when they had such money worries, scandal could be fatal. She shook her head. Everyone in London must know about it by now. Really, she didn't know what to say to him.

Actually, she didn't want to speak to him at all.

She would not normally have noticed the well-dressed man walking quickly towards the corner. But she recognised this one immediately. It was her husband. She knew for certain that he had left the house as soon as she had arrived.

'You're despicable,' she murmured.

'I beg your pardon, ma'am.'

Mrs Darling stepped back and handed Bradley her hat. 'Will you fetch some eau-de-Cologne? I have a headache from the journey.'

'Shall I lay out your tea gown, ma'am?'

'No, thank you. I shall lie down, I think. Please tell Mrs Jenkins I'll have my supper on a tray.'

'Yes, ma'am.'

The door closed. It occurred to Mrs Darling it was odd that her husband should be at home on a weekday in the afternoon. But, then, what did she know about business? She pushed the thought from her head and began to unbutton her blouse.

Three weeks later, Wendy and John kicked a ball back and forth in the garden while Michael hid under a pile of leaves, pretending to be a hedgehog. Neither game lasted very long. After Rosegrove, the garden seemed like something out of a miniature village. There weren't even enough leaves to make a decent pile to hide under and if you kicked your ball too high, it went over the wall into the next-door house. Liza had already had to ask for it back so many times that now she refused to do it again. It was almost more fun to play up in the nursery. At least then John could get on with building his model aeroplane and Wendy could paint the dog sledge she had built for her South Pole Adventurers game. And Michael could make more icebergs. Even Nana had been turned into an honorary huskie. Wendy had made a special paper harness to fit around her neck.

'I've decided to pretend I'm an orphan,' said Wendy to Nana when they were alone in the nursery one afternoon. 'That means both of my parents are dead.'

It'll never work.

'Why shouldn't it work?' demanded Wendy. 'I hate both of them. They might as well be dead.' But even as she spoke, she knew Nana was right. It would be easier if she *could* hate them. Actually, she had tried, but somehow she couldn't make it work, and all she felt was hurt and angry and muddled.

She buried her face in the dog's neck. 'Do you

think I'm going crazy, Nana?' But Nana did not answer.

'Did you enjoy your visit to Rosegrove, Wendy?' asked Mr Darling in a suspiciously pleasant voice.

Wendy stood in the middle of the drawing room. She knew she should look at him but she could not bear to. He was as blotchy and bad-tempered as he had been when they had first returned home.

At the other end of the room, her mother sat on the sofa and stared out of the window. They both looked stiff and uncomfortable. As soon as she had walked through the door, Wendy knew they had been arguing.

'Yes, thank you, Father.'

'Then you've got a funny way of showing it,' snapped her father. He crossed the room and took her chin in his hand. 'Look at me, for heaven's sake. You've barely spoken to anyone except that dog since you got back.'

Wendy opened her mouth but no words came out. It was always the same. First she was angry, then she was too hurt to speak.

'Are you dumb, child?' asked her father.

It was what Lady Cunningham had said in her horrible nightmare. Wendy clenched her hands together and pressed her fingernails hard into her palms. She wasn't about to let her father see her cry.

'I'm not dumb,' she said in the steadiest voice she could manage. 'I –'

'See!' interrupted George Darling. He glared at his wife. 'She's better off staying in the nursery with Michael.'

Wendy felt her stomach turn over. 'Is John going away?'

'Of course not,' said her mother quickly. 'He's not old enough yet. But there's a day school nearby and now, with Nanny Holborn gone, we need to find a governess for you and Michael.'

'Why can't I go to school?'

'I'm not paying for a child who only talks to a dog,' said Mr Darling. 'John will go to day school and we'll shut the dog outside. Then you'll *have* to read your books!'

'But, Father,' cried Wendy, 'I read books all the time. Please don't shut Nana outside.'

'No buts,' snapped Mr Darling. 'I've made up my mind and that's final.'

'There's no need to speak to Wendy like that,' said Mrs Darling in an icy voice. 'It's you who are behaving like a child.'

Wendy was flabbergasted. She had never seen her parents so angry with each other. Her mother sounded as if she despised her father. Could it be that at last she had found out about Lady Cunningham? Or maybe the opposite had happened. Somehow her father had found out about Thomas. But how could he? He hardly ever went to Rosegrove and, when he did, he always found an excuse to leave early. Whatever it was, Wendy wanted to get out of the room as soon as possible. She edged towards the door.

'And just where do you think you're going?' snarled Mr Darling.

'Stop it, George!' snapped Mrs Darling.

'What about me?' shouted Mr Darling suddenly. 'What about *me*!' He turned to Wendy, who was now by the door. 'Oh, for God's sake, go back to the nursery.'

'Wendy!' cried Mrs Darling. She ran across the room and held out her arms. 'Please –'

Wendy pushed her away. 'I hate you! I hate you both!' She wrenched open the door and ran up the stairs.

Wendy wrapped her arms around Nana's neck and sobbed. 'They're going to shut you outside. What will I do without you?'

It doesn't matter where I am. You can always talk to me.

After her outburst in the drawing room, Wendy had been

prepared to be shut in the nursery for the rest of her life. But the next afternoon her mother sent for her and took her to Selfridges to buy a party dress for Christmas. 'I know it's only October, but they already have lovely things in stock.' Now they were sitting in Selfridges' tea room, sipping tea. 'Just the two of us,' said Mrs Darling brightly. 'Isn't this fun.' But they both knew it wasn't. It was uncomfortable and strange.

Wendy tried to think of something to say. Her new blue and silver party dress had been wrapped up in tissue paper and packed into a flat, brown box which was now beside her on the floor. Finally she said, 'Thank you for my dress.'

Mrs Darling laughed awkwardly. 'I had no idea you had grown so much.' Her voice trailed away and she looked down at her hands.

Wendy knew she could make things easier for her mother by talking about the Arabian Nights window displays in the shop or about how much John loved his new school. Instead she finished the last of her ice cream.

'Look here,' said Mrs Darling suddenly, 'I want to talk to you about Father.'

This time Wendy wasn't going to make things easy. 'Why is he being so nasty?'

Mrs Darling touched Wendy's hand. 'Life is very difficult for him just now. He'll be his old self in a short while.' As she said it, she wished she could believe it. He still hadn't told her about the incident at the demonstration and, even though it had happened more than a month ago now, she could not bring herself to confront him. It was easier for them both to live in separate worlds.

Wendy suddenly noticed how thin her mother had become. Her blue eyes looked enormous and her cheekbones were sharp-edged under her greyish-white skin. 'I'm sorry,' she said reluctantly.

'It's your father who should be sorry.' Mrs Darling shook her head and sipped at her tea, even though it must have gone cold.

The chatter and bustle of the tea room made their silence more and more uncomfortable.

'Has something upset you, Wendy? Ever since you hit your head, I feel you're angry with me and I don't know why.'

Wendy could feel herself blushing. It was all she had thought about for weeks now. *Tell her!* said a voice in her head. *Tell her about Thomas and about Father and Lady Cunningham! Tell her and get it over with.* But Wendy told the voice to shut up. Whatever she said, she knew her mother would twist it. She could hear her now: *Don't be ridiculous, dear. That's impossible. You must have imagined it. Really, Wendy, you shouldn't tell lies.*

Suddenly, Wendy had had enough. Why shouldn't her mother answer some questions for a change?

'Why did we have to leave Rosegrove so quickly?'

Mrs Darling looked startled. 'That was ages ago.'

'But why?'

'Your father had an accident.'

'An accident?' cried Wendy. 'What kind of accident? I never saw anything wrong with him.'

Mrs Darling looked as if she was about to burst into tears. 'Why do you hate your father so much?'

Wendy looked into her eyes and was about to tell her when she saw those same eyes looking straight at her from over Thomas's shoulder. And she said, 'Hate Father? Mother! Really! Of course I don't hate him. Sometimes I get cross, that's all.' And when she had finished, she was gasping for air.

'It was too horribilino!' cried Letitia. 'Muddy and dull and *boring*. Saundersbane was dark and cold. Northumberland was *ghastly*. And Cousin Katherine looked like a smelly old camel.' Letitia put her basket on the nursery table. 'She even had a humpback! Anyway, it doesn't matter, because Mama says we need never go there again.'

Wendy laughed despite herself. She had never thought she would be pleased to see Letitia, but even though she had Michael for company, it was lonely in the nursery without John, and Father still hadn't hired a governess.

'Henry said you hit your father with an axe and that's why John's going to school and you aren't,' said Letitia slyly. 'Is that true?'

'Of course it's not. Axes are stupid. I dug an elephant trap in the garden and he fell in.'

Letitia's eyes went round and wide. 'Is that how you got rid of Nanny Holborn?'

Wendy shook her head. 'I filled her knickers up with stones and pushed her in the Round Pond.'

'You didn't?'

'Of course I didn't. I poisoned her Marmite with cyanide.'

'Oh, shut up,' said Letitia crossly. 'I should have known you'd talk nonsense.' She rummaged about in her basket. 'Anyway, that's not why I'm here.' She pulled out a big green cardboard scrapbook. It had POINTERS FOR A PERFECT PARTY written on the cover. 'I wanted to show you this. It's got everything. Even recipes for *puteet*-fours. That's French for little cakes.'

'Why would I want to know about little French cakes?'

'Promise you won't tell anyone.'

'I promise.'

'Cross your heart and hope to die.'

'Yup.'

'Mama's going to throw a surprise party for me.' Letitia's eyes lit up like candles. 'And I need your help.'

'Me?' said Wendy. 'I'm no good at parties. The last one I went to I threw up in a flowerpot and Nanny Holborn had to bring me home.'

Letitia laughed. 'You really are peculiar, aren't you?'

Wendy grinned. 'I like to think so. Anyway, how do you know you're having a party if it's supposed to be a surprise?'

'Mama told me. Well, not *me* exactly.' Letitia squirmed. Wendy could imagine her hiding in the hall with her ear pressed to her mother's sitting-room door. 'Look here,' said Letitia. 'Do you want to hear a secret?'

Wendy pulled a face. 'Not particularly.'

But Letitia wasn't listening. 'Well, I'll tell you,' she cried in a delighted voice. She took a deep breath. 'Last Thursday a policeman came see to Esther.'

Wendy looked up sharply. 'A policeman? She's not in any trouble, is she?'

'Depends on what you call trouble,' said Letitia smugly. ' Mama says she was at that terrible demonstration.'

'What terrible demonstration?'

'In the summer, when you were away. Apparently they

threw stones and smashed windows and everything!' Letitia folded her chubby arms. 'Mama says Esther should go to prison.'

'Was she smashing windows?'

'Hundreds of them. But the policeman was asking about someone else.'

'Who?'

'Aha!' cried Letitia triumphantly. 'That's the secret bit.' She leaned forward and whispered in Wendy's ear. 'It's something to do with Esther and your father.'

'My father!' cried Wendy. 'But he hates suffragettes!'

'Then why was the policeman asking about him?' said Letitia.

'How should I know? Have you told your mother?'

Letitia shook her head. 'How can I?' She fiddled with the cover of her scrapbook.

'You mean you were listening to Esther talking to Sir Alfred?'

'Why shouldn't I listen?' cried Letitia suddenly. 'No one tells me anything! Anyway, I didn't come here to be lectured by you.' She flicked through the scrapbook to a page of pictures. 'Don't want Bible stories. Don't want fairies. *Hate* animals.' Letitia jabbed one page with her finger. 'What about an "Alice in Wonderland" fancy-dress party? I think Alice would suit me.'

But Wendy was hardly listening. Why would a policeman be asking Esther about Father? And it must be something serious if Esther told Sir Alfred.

'What do you think?' said Letitia crossly.

Wendy looked up. 'Sorry. What did you say?'

Letitia clicked her tongue. 'You *really* are stupid. It's so *easy*. I tell *you*. You tell your mother and she tells mine.' She jabbed her finger on the page again. 'Then I get the party I want. Understand?'

'No,' said Wendy. 'Never in a million years.'

* * *

'Can I say good night to Nana?' asked Wendy.

'If you're quick,' said Liza.

Wendy ran down the back stairs and along the stone corridor to the garden door. She was just about to turn the handle when her eye caught sight of a box of old newspapers by the coal-hole door. If the suffragettes really had thrown stones and smashed windows at that demonstration, there might be something about it in the papers. But September was almost two months ago. Surely Mrs Jenkins would have used them by now? Still, it was worth a try. It was the only way she could find out.

Wendy bent down and pulled newspapers out from the bottom of the pile. She couldn't believe it! They were all there and some of the ones for September were perfectly folded, as if her father hadn't even opened them. She flipped through each paper for every day of the last week they had been at Rosegrove. There was nothing. Wendy sighed. It seemed unlikely that Letitia would make up such a story, but you could never be sure. She had been caught out too many times to trust her an inch.

She pulled out one more perfectly folded paper. On the front page was a picture of a crowd of women walking down the Strand, carrying banners. Along the pavement, the shop windows had jagged holes in them. Some of the women were clearly throwing things. Wendy turned the page and saw the words: *Disgraceful Conduct All Round.* Her heart went cold. It was a picture of another crowd of women, but this time there was a man climbing out of a motor car, shaking his fist. She couldn't see his face but that didn't matter. She knew the shape of the car and the high-standing collar of his tartan motoring coat. She even recognised the bobble top on his peaked cap.

It was her father.

She thought of her mother's face, so thin and greyish-white in the tea room. *Your father had an accident.* Wendy ripped up the picture and stuffed the paper back in the pile. Why couldn't her mother tell her the truth for once in her life? She yanked open the back door and crawled into Nana's kennel.

Nana licked Wendy's face as she curled up beside her.

So there you are. I was wondering when you'd come.

13

Liza bent down on her knees in front of Nana's kennel. It smelled warm and musty. Wendy lay curled up like a baby in the straw beside the big black dog. She was asleep, but there was no peace on her face. Her brows were drawn together and her fists were clenched, crossed over her chest. She stirred in her sleep and put her arms around Nana's neck.

'What's going on, Nana?' whispered Liza with a lump in her throat. 'They've all gone mad.'

As gently as she could, she pulled Wendy out of the straw.

'Please. Let me stay,' murmured Wendy sleepily. 'Please, Liza.' She tried to twist out of her grasp.

'Come along now, Wendy,' whispered Liza. 'Everyone's been looking for you. Now hurry before we all get into more trouble.'

Wendy shivered. It was dark. 'Are Mother and Father angry with me?'

'No, no,' said Liza. What was the point of telling the child the truth? She squeezed Wendy's hand. 'You look like a scarecrow with all that straw in your hair.'

When they reached the front hall, Wendy pulled back. Why on earth was Liza going up the main stairs? She knew it was forbidden.

'The electric's bust on the back stairs,' hissed Liza, dragging her forward. 'It's pitch black.'

'I'd rather go that way. Please, Liza.'

But Liza had made up her mind. 'Come along now,' she said. Mr and Mrs Darling were in their rooms. Besides, she'd very nearly fallen down the back stairs on her way to the garden. She pulled Wendy forward.

They were halfway up the first flight of stairs when Mr Darling walked onto the landing, wearing his dressing gown. He walked across to his wife's door.

'I want to talk you,' he said in a strange, slurred voice. He pushed open the door and went inside.

Liza's face went white. She dragged Wendy quickly on up the stairs but Wendy was completely awake now. Behind the closed door, her parents' voices rose and fell. Liza and Wendy ran up the stairs. When they were on the nursery landing, a great shout rang through the house.

'Asleep in the dog house?' bellowed Mr Darling. 'What kind of behaviour is that? The brat's mad. She belongs in Colney Hatch with her big bloody brother.' He slammed Mrs Darling's bedroom door. A Chinese porcelain jar on the landing table crashed to the floor.

Another door slammed and the landing went dark.

Wendy gasped in the darkness. What was he talking about? She didn't have an older brother. John was younger than her and he wasn't mad. Wendy stared at Liza, looking for comfort. But instead Liza flushed scarlet, lowered her eyes and stared at the floor. Wendy's head began to spin. She felt her mouth drop open and her hands fall to her sides.

'Your father's drunk, Wendy,' said Liza. 'He doesn't know what he's saying.'

It was what Wendy had wanted her to say, but it was too late. Liza's voice sounded forced and odd.

She knew that what she had just heard was true and that Liza was lying to her.

That night Wendy felt she would never sleep. She told herself again and again that she had a big bloody brother who was mad and at somewhere called Colney Hatch. But she might as well have been speaking Chinese, because she didn't understand what she was telling herself. Even so, she'd heard her father say it and it didn't matter if he was drunk. The look on Liza's face had told her it was true. And if it was true, then what was Colney Hatch? Was it a place for mad people?

The thoughts kept bouncing around her mind like rubber balls. She tried to think what she knew about mad people. And the more she thought about it, the more she realised that she didn't know anything.

One Christmas at Rosegrove she had climbed up to the fruit store to help Mrs Fielding gather apples for a pudding. She remembered reaching into the wooden box in the corner of the dark attic and feeling her fingers sink into a mouldy mush. 'All it takes is one bad apple,' Mrs Fielding had said. Then she dragged the box into the day-light and, sure enough, all the other apples were rotten. Now Wendy wondered about that one bad apple. Is that what happened to mad people? Did they catch madness off someone else?

Her thoughts went round and round and up and down. At last she fell into a jerky dream. Her father was standing in a circus ring, wearing a ringmaster's hat. All around him there were mad people in cages, shrieking and howling. Her father cracked his whip and his face split into a terrible smile. 'Welcome to Colney Hatch,' he cried, and beckoned her into the ring.

George Darling folded a spotted blue silk handkerchief into his top pocket. His fingers shook as he wrapped his tie into a wide knot. He had cut himself shaving.

The house was silent as he walked down the stairs to the hallway. The November sky was black and cloudy beyond the landing window. It was going to rain. He rummaged in his pocket for change for a cab. It wouldn't do to arrive at his club with mud on his trousers. Not that the other fellows were very friendly these days. Not since that bloody newspaper story. As for Victoria Cunningham, she had cut him dead on the street. He counted his coins and his eye caught sight of a broken jar lying on the carpet. *Clumsy servants.* A picture flashed through his mind. He was standing outside his wife's bedroom. He had to talk to her. He couldn't stand it any more. Broke, no job, hounded by the police . . . She was brushing her hair. Then, when she turned round, the look on her face was the same look that was on Wendy's face. It was clear. He disgusted her.

George Darling caught sight of his reflection in the mirror. His eyes were bloodshot and his skin hung from his cheeks in lard-coloured folds. But he knew it wasn't just his appearance that disgusted her. Over the past few weeks, he had noticed small things disappear. Two exquisitely carved silver pheasants from the dining-room table, a jade frog from the mantelpiece in the drawing room and, most shaming of all, her father's wedding present to her – an enamelled gold egg, decorated with lilies of the valley in pearls and rose diamonds. He knew she had pawned them. Why else would the butcher give him a friendly nod or the livery boy whistle when he passed? She had paid off her household bills the only way she could. No wonder he disgusted her. The extent of his failure made him feel sick and miserable. Yet he was angry too. Why should he take the blame for everything? It wasn't his fault the stock market had plummeted. It wasn't his fault those idiot women had chosen to demonstrate on the one afternoon he had taken out the motor. If only the gearbox hadn't jammed into reverse. He could have driven away and he'd still have a job. *Why me?* he howled inside his head. *Why does this have to happen to me?*

At the bottom of the stairs, Alice looked up, startled. She bobbed and backed into a doorway with a dustpan and brush in her hand. She could smell the stale whisky on his breath.

'Nasty old soak,' muttered Alice as she watched him put on his overcoat, take an umbrella from the stand and stumble down the front steps into the cold, grey drizzle. Then she climbed the stairs to sweep up the broken jar.

* * *

Nellie stood on the front doorstep of the Cunninghams' house. 'I'm sorry, Miss Wendy, Letitia's still in bed. Would you like to call later?'

Liza tugged at Wendy's arm. If it hadn't been for last night, she would never have agreed to call on the Cunninghams so early. But she wanted to do something kind for Wendy and this was what the girl had asked for. 'Come along now, Wendy. You've had your answer.'

But Wendy didn't move. It wasn't Letitia she wanted to see. 'Is Esther at home, Nellie?'

'For goodness' sake,' said Liza crossly. 'You can't go around disturbing people before breakfast time.' She bent down and whispered in Wendy's ear, 'If it's about that nonsense last night –'

'No, no,' replied Wendy. Her face looked flushed and hectic. 'It's about Letitia's surprise party.'

'Promise?'

'Promise,' said Wendy, who was past caring whether

she lied or told the truth. She'd do whatever it took to speak to Esther. Esther was the only person whom she could trust to tell her the truth.

Liza sucked in her breath. 'I'll come back in twenty minutes.'

'No need for that,' said Nellie, who had been watching them both carefully. 'We'll bring her home when she's ready.' And she gave Liza a little lift of the chin that said, *I'm a friend of Mrs Jenkins and we both know what's going on in your house.*

A minute later, Wendy stood in the Cunninghams' front hall with her back pressed against a door, eyeing the jungle of bamboos nervously, as if some animal might jump out and sink its teeth into her throat.

'Don't worry dearie,' said Nellie, winking. 'Lady Cunningham never gets up before eleven.'

At that moment, Esther walked down the stairs. 'Hello, Wendy. What a surprise!'

'Will you take me for a walk?'

'Now?' said Esther in a puzzled voice. 'It's raining.'

'Please, Esther,' said Wendy desperately. 'It's almost stopped.'

Esther hesitated, then pulled on her hat and coat. 'A walk would be lovely,' she said. 'We'll take an umbrella. The park, do you think?'

'Where would you like to go?' asked Esther, pulling up the collar of her long blue coat as they walked through the park gates. The rain had stopped but the wind was wet and cold.

Wendy didn't care where they went, so she said the first thing that came into her head. 'How about the Round Pond? I haven't been there for ages.'

Esther smiled. 'Off we jolly well go, then. Come, take my hand. You must be freezing.'

Esther felt Wendy's small hand slip into her gloved

hand and wrapped her fingers around it. From the moment she had seen Wendy in the hall, she was sure that somehow the child had found out about her father. But how? She had been away in the country. And even though the story had been in the papers, it was inconceivable that Wendy's parents had said anything and she knew her own papa and stepmother had been careful not mention it in front of Letitia or Henry. Whatever the case, it was still not definite that the police would press charges. Esther had made it clear she would not give evidence against him and had repeated it to the officer who interviewed her the other day.

'John's learning Greek at his school,' said Wendy as they walked past the Albert Hall. 'I hope my governess can teach me.'

'When is she coming?'

'I don't know.'

Esther looked puzzled. 'So what do you do all day?'

'Oh, I read my encyclopaedias and teach Michael his numbers. Letitia told me about her surprise party. I don't like parties much.' They crossed Kensington Gore and walked through the Palace Gates.

'Wendy,' asked Esther at last, 'did you ask me here to talk about your father?'

Wendy shook her head. 'Not particularly, but Letitia told me and I found a picture in the newspaper.' She kicked the ground with her boot. 'I knew straight away it was Father. Do you think he'll go to prison?'

'Sometimes I could strangle Letitia,' said Esther angrily. 'It's impossible to have a conversation without her lurking at the door. Of course your father won't go to prison. They might even drop the charges against him. That's why the policeman came to see me. I was a witness.'

But Wendy didn't seem to be listening. She was running her hands along the railings and dodging the cracks in the pavement.

'So it's not your father, then,' said Esther. Sometimes she wondered if she would ever understand children.

Wendy shook her head. 'You've got to promise not to tell anyone.'

'Not a soul.'

Wendy chewed her lip. Now that the moment had finally arrived, she didn't know where to start. 'What's Colney Hatch? I mean, what's it got to do with mad people?'

It was just about the last thing Esther was expecting to hear. 'Colney Hatch is a hospital,' she said. 'It's where they look after lunatics.'

'Is madness a disease?'

Esther frowned. 'Sort of a disease. But it's a disease of the mind.'

'So you can catch it?'

'Good Lord, no!' Esther looked down at Wendy's face. 'What's the matter, Wendy? Has someone been saying horrible things to you?' Someone like Letitia, thought Esther to herself.

'No, no, it's not that.' Wendy thought hard. 'So can mad people get better?'

'Of course they can. That's what hospitals like Colney Hatch are for.'

'Is Colney Hatch in London?' asked Wendy as casually as she could.

'Just outside,' replied Esther. 'Not too far away.'

Wendy's face lit up. 'So I could get there in a cab?'

Esther laughed. 'You could get there any way you liked. If it was me I'd take the omnibus to Victoria and change.'

'I think a cab would be better,' said Wendy thoughtfully. 'It would be faster and less complicated.'

Good God, thought Esther to herself, the child's serious. She began to regret her promise to keep the conversation secret. 'Wendy, I think you should tell me what is going on.'

So Wendy thought up a lie and she discovered it was terribly easy. 'I heard Alice tell Liza she had a big brother in Colney Hatch and that she'd never seen him because her parents sent him away.' Wendy looked up. 'Do you think that's true, Esther? Would people really send their child away? Even if he was mad?' She swallowed. 'Wouldn't they love him enough to keep him?'

'Well, I'm afraid it does happen,' said Esther in an uncomfortable voice. She frowned as she tried to pick her words carefully. 'But it doesn't mean Alice's parents didn't love their son. Probably just that they couldn't afford to keep him and look after their other children as well. Does Alice have many brothers and sisters?'

Wendy had no idea. She thought of Aunt Emily's photograph. 'Eleven,' she said in a small voice.

But inside an angry voice was shouting. Mother and Father could have afforded to keep her big brother, whoever he was. They didn't have to send him away. So why did they do it? And even as she asked herself the question, she knew the answer. Her mother would have kept him. But her father . . . Only the best was good enough for her father.

'Do you think it's wrong to hate your father?'

'Does Alice hate her father?'

Wendy nodded.

'I don't think it's wrong,' said Esther. 'But I do think it's sad. Perhaps Alice's father hates himself more than she hates him and she just hasn't noticed.' Esther shrugged. 'She'll never know and he'll never tell her. *Very* sad.'

But Wendy was only half listening. She was thinking of her big brother and making a plan. Her father always said Darling was an unusual name. That meant it would be easy to find her brother at the hospital. Then she'd take him to Rosegrove. Uncle Arthur would look after him, even if her parents didn't want to.

'Oh, my goodness!' cried Esther, looking at her pocket watch. 'I must go! Our leader, Mrs Pankhurst, is speaking at a meeting in Shoreditch and I don't want to miss her.'

Esther took Wendy's hand and they quickly crossed over to Kensington Park Gardens. 'If I leave you here, will you promise to go straight back?' Esther looked at her watch again. 'It's only five minutes away and you won't have to cross any roads.'

Wendy squeezed Esther's hand. 'You go to your meeting. I'll run home all the way. I promise.'

'Are you sure?'

Wendy nodded. 'Look! There's a cab! I'll whistle for it if you like.' She grinned. 'I'm an expert wolf-whistler.'

Five minutes later, Esther was gone and Wendy stood on her own on the pavement. If she hadn't whistled for Esther's cab, she would never have thought of whistling for one herself. Because that was the part of her plan she wasn't sure of. Would a cab driver stop for a young girl on her own? And then would he take her all the way to Colney Hatch?

A cab trotted around the corner. It was now or never. Wendy put two fingers in her mouth and whistled.

The cab slowed down as if the driver was trying to make up his mind. Then he stopped.

'Where to, miss?'

'Colney Hatch, please.'

'Colney Hatch?' cried the driver. 'You'd be better to take a tram to Finchley, then change to the bus.'

Wendy's heart hammered in her chest. 'But that would take too long,' she said in her firmest voice. Then she had an idea. 'My mother is desperately ill. I've got the money. Father gave it to me specially.' It was extraordinary. Telling lies was so easy.

The driver looked down at the little girl's serious face. 'What's your name, miss?'

'Peggy Crocker. I live in Kensington Crescent.' Wendy put on her most pleading face. 'Please take me.'

The driver thought of the fare. It was a long way to Colney Hatch and he could do with the money. Still, it was most unusual, but at least now he knew the girl's name. 'Someone taking you back?'

'My father.'

He made up his mind. 'Hop in, then, miss,' he said, pulling open the doors. 'Mind your dress on them wheels.'

Wendy sat back on the brown leather seats and felt the cab jolt forward over the cobbles. She was so excited, she could hardly breathe. Very soon she would be sitting in a cab just like this one. Now she knew she could make a driver pick her up, there was nothing to stop her carrying out her plan.

At the end of the street, she banged on the cab roof and leaned out over the front doors. 'Stop! Stop!' she shouted.

The cab driver pulled up. 'Is something the matter, miss?'

Wendy undid the doors and climbed down onto the street. 'I'm sorry,' she said. 'I've changed my mind.'

'Changed your mind?' cried the cab driver angrily. In his head, he'd already spent the fare for the trip. 'You can't do that!' He tied up the horse's reins and heaved himself down from the cab. 'Sounds like you belong in Colney Hatch yourself!'

But Wendy didn't hear him. She was already halfway down the street.

'Nana's back!' cried Michael as soon as Wendy came through the nursery door.

'I don't know what you told Father,' said John proudly, 'but it worked.'

Across the room, Liza was mending a nightshirt.

Wendy stared at her brother. 'Why aren't you in school?'

'I felt ill,' said John. 'Not that it's any of your business. So what did you say to Father?'

'I told him the truth,' said Wendy. She knew that Liza was listening, so she gave her something to hear. 'I told him that I loved Nana better than him and that if he didn't like it, he could send me away.'

John stared at his sister aghast. 'You didn't!'

'Then what did Father say?' asked Michael thoughtfully.

Wendy looked up and saw Liza was staring at her open-mouthed. 'He said I was mad,' replied Wendy simply. She went over to Nana's basket and wrapped her arms around the dog's neck. 'And maybe I am.' As she spoke, she tried to catch Liza's eye to see how she was reacting, but this time Liza refused to look at her.

Nana turned her head and licked Wendy's ear.

Careful now or you'll cut yourself.

* * *

The following Saturday, Wendy crept into her mother's room. It was mid-morning and she knew that Bradley was washing her mother's hair and that it always took at least half an hour to rinse it clean. A gold evening dress and an embroidered purple silk jacket lay over the arm of a chair. Vaguely, Wendy remembered a time when she would have buried her face in them and breathed in the last traces of perfume, imagining that she was as tall and beautiful and graceful as her mother. Now the idea made her want to be sick.

She went across to the dressing table. Her mother kept money in the middle drawer – Wendy had seen her take out a flat black leather box and count out banknotes. She opened the drawer. It was full of little velvet-lined ring boxes and silver powder pots. She felt around at the back. Sure enough, there was the flat leather box. She pulled it out and, without a moment of guilt, took all the notes and coins she could find. It had to be enough to get her to Colney Hatch.

'What have you got in your hand?' asked John as Wendy walked into the nursery.

Wendy looked up with a start. 'I thought you were playing with Henry.'

'I was,' said John. 'What have you got in your hand?' he repeated.

Wendy thought quickly. The last thing she wanted was to make John suspicious. 'Money for our shopkeepers game,' she said, grinning a dreadful false grin. She spread the money into a fan and waved it back and forth. 'I stole it from Mother's room so we could play with the real thing.'

'Liar,' said John. He seemed particularly cheerful. 'You painted them, didn't you?'

'How did you guess?'

'Because I'm incredibly clever,' cried John, leaping into the middle of the room and dancing around the floor. 'Do you want to know why I'm not playing with Henry Cunningham?'

'Let me guess. He tried to stab you with a penknife?'

John laughed. 'Not this time. It's because he says he's too grand to play with us any more.'

'And why is Henry so grand all of a sudden?' As she spoke, Wendy folded the banknotes and hid them in the toy cupboard.

'Because the cousin in Northumberland died and left everything to Sir Alfred. Henry says he's going to ask for a pair of Purdeys for his birthday.'

'Purdeys?'

'Shotguns,' said John. 'Don't you know *anything*?'

'But Henry can't hit a barn door,' said Wendy. 'Letitia told me.'

'That's not what Henry says,' replied John. 'And Letitia wants you to know that she'll still ask you over to play when they move to their new house.'

'What new house?'

John shrugged. 'I don't know. Letitia said it was

bigger than ours. In Portman Square or somewhere.'

'She'll like that,' said Wendy. But she wasn't thinking about Letitia. She was thinking about the money in the toy cupboard and the cab to Colney Hatch.

Letitia was sitting on her mother's lap. She buried her face in her lacy blouse. 'Will our new house have lots and lots of rooms, Mama?'

'Hundreds,' replied Lady Cunningham, kissing her daughter's curly black hair.

'And will we have lots and lots of servants?'

'Thousands,' laughed her mother. 'And you will have your very own maid.'

'*Delicious*,' cried Letitia, snuggling closer. 'And will you buy me lots and lots of dresses?'

Lady Cunningham tilted up her daughter's chin with her finger and smiled a wide, full-lipped smile. 'One for every day of the year, my darling.'

Letitia was so delighted all she could do was squirm.

There was a knock on the door.

Lady Cunningham sat up and eased Letitia off her lap. 'Now, off you go, my little princess. That will be the French *couturière* to show me her new patterns.' She smoothed her hair and straightened her blouse.

Letitia gazed at her mother with wide, glistening eyes. 'Oooh, Mama,' she whispered. '*Couturière.* Is she really *French*?' The door opened and Sir Alfred Cunningham stepped into the room.

'Alfred!' Lady Cunningham stood up hurriedly. 'My dear! I'm sorry, I was expecting Madame Parmentier.'

'Dearest Papa!' cried Letitia in her brand-new heiress's voice. She ran across the room and wrapped her arms around her father's waist. 'I'm so *thrilled* about Portman Square.'

Sir Alfred looked down at his daughter. There was a smug, fat expression on her face as if she had been eating expensive chocolates all morning. He found himself feeling mildly sickened. 'Portman Square? What on earth are you talking about?' He unwound his daughter's arms and put them firmly by her sides. 'Run along to the nursery, Letitia,' he snapped. 'Nanny is waiting for you.'

Papa never talked like this. Letitia turned, horrified, and stared at her mother. Lady Cunningham's face was not glossy and excited any more. It was blank and rigid.

'But, Mama –'

'No buts,' said Sir Alfred angrily. 'Do what you're told for once in your life.'

Letitia went bright red.

'I said *go!*' cried Sir Alfred.

She turned and ran from the room.

'You mustn't be cross with the child, Alfred. She's over-excited.' Lady Cunningham looked into her husband's stern grey face and forced a smooth smile. 'We all are.'

Sir Alfred did not return the smile. 'Who told Letitia we were moving to Portman Square? Henry was spouting the same nonsense when I spoke to him this morning.'

Lady Cunningham frowned. 'I understood that once that ghastly barrack in Northumberland –'

'Ghastly barrack?' said Sir Alfred in a cold voice. 'Is that what you call Saundersbane?'

'Barrack, house, palace. What does it matter?' Lady Cunningham turned and checked her reflection in the mirror. She had quite recovered herself. Alfred was just being silly. She didn't want to appear out of sorts when Madame Parmentier arrived.

'It matters rather a lot to me,' said her husband slowly.

'I'm sorry if I've offended you,' said Lady Cunningham. 'Now, if you will excuse me, I have an appointment.'

At that moment, the door opened and Nellie came in.

'Madame Parmentier to see Lady Cunningham.'

'Tell her to go away,' said Sir Alfred. 'Lady Cunningham is engaged.'

Looking quickly between the two angry faces, Nellie could hardly contain her delight. She was to take tea with Mrs Jenkins this very afternoon and there would be much to tell. 'Yes, sir,' she said. The door closed.

'How dare you humiliate me in front of the servants?' cried Lady Cunningham furiously. 'What *can* be the matter with you?'

'Yes, I imagine you are quite an authority on humiliation,' said Sir Alfred.

The packet of letters addressed to his wife from George Darling had arrived in the post some time before. He didn't read them. One look told him everything he needed to know. At first he couldn't believe that his wife would be unfaithful to him. Then, once he had accepted the truth, he remembered all those flushed-faced, excited accounts of expeditions in George Darling's motor car and his anger turned into a rage that hurt as if a knife had been twisted in his gut. He locked the letters in his desk and gave himself a fortnight to decide what he would do.

Lady Cunningham felt her hands go clammy. 'I don't know what you're talking about.'

'You know perfectly well.' Sir Alfred walked to his wife's dressing table and opened her jewellery box. He held up two pearl earrings set in bright yellow gold and surrounded by rubies. 'Your mother's, you said.'

'Yes.' She heard the tremor in her voice.

'Since when has George Darling been your mother?'

There was a long, deathly silence.

Lady Cunningham stared down at the wedding ring on her finger. Her mind chattered at her. She had many friends whose husbands wouldn't care. As long as everyone kept up the usual show. One did, in society . . .

But she knew Sir Alfred wasn't like that.

'Very well,' she said. 'How long have you known?'

'That's not important.' His voice was hard and without pity.

'It's over, Alfred,' she said. 'You must believe me.'

'Of course, it's over. He's ruined and disgraced.'

Lady Cunningham forced herself to say the words that terrified her most. 'Do you intend to divorce me?'

Sir Alfred sat down in a chair. His wife's full-lipped face suddenly looked heavy and coarse. He closed his eyes. 'I would if it wasn't for the children . . . How *could* you, Victoria? The man's an oaf.'

'I fell in love with his car.' Lady Cunningham's voice was so low he could barely hear. 'I can't explain it.' But she could. She remembered the smell of oil on his motoring cloak, the judder of the engine and then the dizzy thrill as the world flashed past her eyes. She sat down and let her head fall forwards on her chest, so she would not have to look at him as he pronounced sentence on her. 'What do you want to do?' she asked dully.

'We shall be moving to Saundersbane.'

Lady Cunningham gasped, as if someone had thrown a glass of water in her face. 'But, Alfred, that's impossible! I'd – I'd go mad!'

'Then you must choose between madness and divorce.'

Lady Cunningham stood up and walked over to the window. A shiny grey Rolls-Royce was waiting in the street. She watched as a woman in an ermine-trimmed cloak climbed into the back. She would be leaving all this for a damp house in a sea of mud with only red-nosed squires and their drab, stupid wives to talk to. The prospect made her feel physically ill. But she knew she had no choice. The scandal of a divorce was inconceivable.

She stood up with her shoulders back and looked Sir Alfred in the face. 'When do you want to leave?'

'I want to be there for Christmas.'

'Christmas!' cried Lady Cunningham, aghast. 'But I've booked seats at all the pantomimes and Letitia and Henry have been asked to Lady Sheffield's children's party. Letitia will be so disappointed.'

'Then the sooner you tell them the better.' Sir Alfred stood up and rang the servants' bell.

'Yes, sir.'

'Tell Nanny to send the children down immediately.'

'Yes, sir.' Nellie bobbed, eyes lowered, but her heart surged in her chest. She didn't have to look at their faces this time. The atmosphere in the room told her everything she wanted to know. Goodness, what a tea it was going to be!

Wendy stood with John and Michael in Mrs Kettle's High-Class Confectionery shop. They had begged Liza to let them look while she bought mending wool and ribbon down the street. But as soon as Liza was out of the door, Wendy handed her brothers thrupence each. 'Ask Mrs Kettle for what you want. And hurry. Liza'll be back in five minutes.'

'Thrupence!' cried John in amazement.

Wendy stared at him hard. 'I've been saving up my pocket money for ages and I don't know what else to do with it.'

As she said it, she felt sad and confused, not because she had decided that tomorrow was the day she was leaving, but because, as they had walked down Seaton Street to the haberdasher's shop, they had passed a pawn-shop and Wendy had recognised a china figure from her mother's dressing table. It was a shepherdess dressed in blue, wearing a lacy bonnet and holding a bunch of rosebuds in her hands. The shepherdess had always reminded her of her mother and the rosebuds were so beautifully painted you could almost smell their perfume. She had no idea why her mother would have pawned it. But she was sure it had something to do with all the unhappiness in the house. Wendy wondered if her father had seen it there too. A couple of days before, he had brought them each back a bag of sweets from Mrs Kettle's shop. Not that he'd given them the sweets himself – Liza had handed them out. Wendy knew he was probably feeling guilty for knocking over Mother's porcelain jar. Everyone in the house knew that it was him who had done it. Anyway, she was sure he would have noticed the china shepherdess. It was difficult to miss in the middle of the window.

'Sure you're not going to change your mind?'

'What's that?'

John stared at his sister. His mouth was watering so much he could barely speak without drooling. 'About the thrupence?'

'I'm sure.'

John shook his head as if his sister was mad and began ordering bull's-eyes and liquorice sticks and sherbet lemons as fast as possible.

Michael had already asked an assistant for as many wine gums as thrupence would buy. Michael was notoriously single-minded when it came to sweets.

Wendy watched as they handed over the money and crammed their pockets with little paper bags. So far everything was going according to plan. Her idea was to give John and Michael a treat before she left to take her new brother down to Rosegrove, as she didn't know when she would see them again. Wendy hadn't quite worked out how she would let her uncle know when they arrived, but she could always sort that out at the station. The important thing was to get there.

Five minutes later, Liza beckoned from the street. 'I've just met Nanny George,' she said to Wendy. 'Apparently Letitia is asking to see you.'

Wendy's face fell. 'Do I have to, Liza? I was going to play South Pole Adventurers with John this afternoon.'

'And with me!' cried Michael. 'I made the icebergs, remember!'

Liza sighed. 'I'm sorry, Wendy. I don't want to make you do something you don't want to, but Nanny George was very . . . well, insistent.'

Wendy looked at Liza's uncomfortable face. Liza was more of a friend than her Nanny. She'd been kind and Wendy didn't want to seem ungrateful.

'Please, Wendy. I did say you'd go.'

'How long do I have to stay?'

'I'll collect you in half an hour.' Liza smiled. 'Tell you what, why don't I buy you all some sweets? Will that make it better?' To her amazement, Michael burst out laughing.

* * *

'I'm going to kill myself, Wendy,' sobbed Letitia. 'They'll find me all dead and waxen and –' She sniffed. 'Will I be puffy?'

Wendy shook her head. 'Nope. You'll be stiff, though.'

'You think it's funny, don't you?' wailed Letitia. 'How would you like to live in a cold, dusty house? There's nothing in Northumberland except mud.'

'There will be snow at Christmas,' said Wendy, as kindly as she could.

'Who needs snow?' Letitia kicked over a chair. 'I'd rather go to prison. At least it would be in London.' She paused and looked sideways at Wendy. 'What do you mean about going stiff?'

'It's called rigor mortis,' said Wendy. 'When you die your body goes sort of hard.'

'You mean if I held a bunch of red roses, no one would be able to pull them from my fingers?'

'Something like that.'

'Mmmm.'

'It's rather jolly living in the country,' said Wendy. 'You could have a pony. You'd look lovely in a veil,' she added.

'I don't want a pony,' shouted Letitia. 'And veils are for old ladies. I want a big house in Portman Square.' Her swollen eyes turned mean. 'If I kill myself, then Mama will be so sorry, she'll have to kill herself too. And it'll serve her right for lying to me.'

'And how are you going to kill yourself?' said Wendy.

'Huh,' snapped Letitia. 'You don't know anything, do you? It's easy. All I have to do is swallow Mama's laudanum.'

Wendy went white. 'You're lying. Your mother doesn't have laudanum.'

'Of course she does,' said Letitia in a nasty voice. 'She calls it cough medicine.'

'Listen to me, Letitia!' cried Wendy. 'Laudanum's

really dangerous. You mustn't even think about it.'

But Letitia wasn't listening. 'Promise me one thing,' she said in a dreamy voice.

'What?'

'Promise me you'll sew black ribbon through your knickers.'

Wendy stared at Letitia as if she had gone completely mad. '*What?*'

'It's what people do when someone important dies.' Letitia dabbed her eyes with a self-pitying handkerchief. 'I'm going to lie down now. It was good of you to see me.' And she glided out of the nursery like a ghost.

Wendy lay in bed and relived again and again the moment she had climbed into the cab. It had been so easy. 'Take me to Colney Hatch, please.' Then in her mind streets passed by as they went further and further north. And, just when she thought the journey would never end, she heard the driver call down, 'We're here, miss!'

Now came the part she had been keeping to last. It was when the nurse appeared, smiling. 'Darling! Ah, yes! An unusual name. Come with me. Your brother will be so pleased to see you.'

Of course, John and Michael would be sad that she had gone. Wendy tossed and turned. Everytime she tried to imagine her new brother's face, Letitia, dead and white, floated into her mind. Blast Letitia! Trust her to ruin things.

'John, are you asleep?'

'Almost. What is it?'

'Letitia said she was going to kill herself.'

John grunted. 'Henry told me. I wouldn't believe a word she says.' He rolled over in his bed.

'But what if she really does and I don't warn someone?'

'Good riddance to bad rubbish,' said John crossly.

'Anyway, all they cause is trouble. I'm glad they're moving.'

'Do you think I should tell Mother?'

'That they're moving?'

'No! About Letitia.'

'She'd think you were mad.' He pulled up his bedclothes. 'Leave me alone so I can go to sleep.'

It was the word mad that did it. They'd sent her big brother to Colney Hatch because he was mad. And if her mother really wanted to keep him, she could have put up a fight and not let Father get his own way, like he always did. Then and there, Wendy decided not to go downstairs and tell her mother. Even so, the more she thought about the bottle of laudanum by Lady Cunningham's bedside, the more worried and angry she became. It was exactly the sort of stupid thing that Letitia would do . . .

Wendy had to tell someone and suddenly she thought of a brilliant way to do it. She slipped out of bed and put on her dressing gown. Liza wasn't in the nursery.

Wendy

Nowadays, no one seemed to care whether Wendy wandered about at night or not. She walked over the linoleum floor to the painted wooden desk where Nanny Holborn had kept the paper and envelopes. Then she sat on the padded chair by the fire and wrote.

Letitia is planning to drink her mother's laudanum and kill herself.

Wendy folded the paper and opened the nursery door. Then she crept down the corridor to the top of the stairs. Everything was quiet. All she had to do was run down, push the letter under her mother's door and run back up again. Then, the next morning, it wouldn't matter, because she'd be gone. Wendy had decided to beg Uncle Arthur to let her stay with her big brother, and she was sure he'd say yes when he found out the truth.

Wendy took a deep breath and started down the stairs.

'Preposterous!' shouted her father.

'I think not,' snapped her mother.

Wendy was halfway down the stairs. She crouched

on the steps and made herself as small as she could. If her mother's door opened now, she was bound to be seen.

'Who else would steal money from my jewellery box?' said her mother's voice. 'You're the one that's broke.' Wendy clutched the stair rail to stop herself falling forward. If only it was light, she could go to Colney Hatch now, this minute.

'I may be broke,' said her father in a desperate voice, 'but *please* don't accuse me of being a thief. Anyone could have taken it. The maids. The children. The bloody dog, for God's sake!'

'Don't be ridiculous.' Her mother's voice sounded tired. 'Give it back and we'll forget all about it.'

'You are quite mad.' Her father's voice sounded hurt but nasty. 'Perhaps you should join your son at Rosegrove? I'm sure the saintly Arthur could find a place for another lunatic.'

'Thomas is not a lunatic,' cried Mrs Darling in a choked voice. 'He's our son.' Her voice broke into sobs. 'And I miss him, George. I miss him so much.'

Wendy clutched the banisters and rocked from side to side. Behind the door, her mother's sobs grew louder and louder until her voice turned into a long shuddering howl.

'Oh, dear God,' said her father. 'How has this happened to us?' And his voice was so low Wendy could hardly hear it.

Wendy's thoughts moved heavily around her head like big silver fish swimming slowly in a pond. She had to keep them slow. It was the only way she could try to understand. She felt her heart would burst. Because now she realised that she had got everything wrong. Now she understood why her mother had been crying when she kissed Thomas. He was her son, and she loved and missed him more than Wendy could ever imagine.

Wendy sat on the stairs and held her head in her hands. After a long, long time, she crept back to bed.

The next morning at breakfast Liza handed Wendy a letter. 'It's for you. Alice found it on the doormat.'

Wendy stared at the blotched black handwriting and a horrible hot feeling washed over her.

'Who's it from?' asked John with a mouth full of porridge.

'Letitia.' Wendy ripped open the envelope and pulled out the sheet of paper inside. A black line had been drawn around the edges.

The Last Rekwest of Letitia Honoria Cunningham.

Dear Wendy,

By the time you read this I will probably be dead. Please tell them to scatter my remains as near as possible to the Ritz Hotel.

Your dead friend,

Letitia

'What's Letitia got to say?' asked John.

'One egg or two?' asked Liza.

'Two please,' said John.

Michael held up one finger.

'Good Lord, Wendy,' cried Liza. 'You're as grey as your porridge.'

John put down his spoon and leaned over to read the letter.

'Oh, no, she's at it again.'

'But what if it's true?' cried Wendy. 'What if we've got it wrong?'

John and Michael watched in astonishment as Wendy threw the letter on the table and burst into tears.

Liza couldn't bear it any more. The poor child was coming to the end of her tether. Liza's face went bright red and she banged down the plate of soft-boiled eggs so hard they jumped out of their cups and rolled onto the floor.

'Why are you angry?' cried Michael.

'I'm not angry!' shouted Liza. She turned away and wiped her nose with her sleeve.

Michael turned to John. 'Why's Liza crying?'

John shook his head. He had absolutely no idea what was happening, except that the soft-boiled eggs he had been looking forward to lay in two yellow puddles on the floor. He picked up the letter and held it out to Liza.

'It's no good showing me that,' snapped Liza. 'You know I can't read.'

John stood up. 'I'll get mother,' he said.

'Your mother's not here,' said Liza. 'She went out with your father early this morning.' She let out a deep breath. 'Tell me what the letter says.'

John looked at Wendy, but she shook her head. 'It says Letitia's dead,' he said. 'Yesterday she told Henry she was going to steal her mother's laudanum and swallow the lot.' He looked up at Liza. 'What's laudanum?'

Liza shrieked and grabbed her coat from the stand. 'Come with me, Wendy. John and Michael, you stay here, and for heaven's sake don't do anything foolish.'

'Can we have our eggs?' asked Michael.

But Liza and Wendy were already halfway down the stairs.

Five minutes later, Liza was banging on the Cunninghams' front door as hard as she could.

Nellie pulled open the door. 'Goodness gracious, Liza!' she cried. 'You'll wake the dead with your banging. Do you realise what time it is?'

'Quick, Nellie,' cried Liza. 'Call the doctor! Letitia has swallowed her mother's laudanum.'

Nellie stared at Liza as if she was mad. 'What are you talking about?'

Wendy held out the letter. 'This came this morning.' Her voice cracked.

'For heaven's sake, come into the hall. You'll catch your death of cold.'

'Nellie!' Liza almost shouted. 'This is an *emergency!*'

Nellie looked down at the letter. 'Humph,' she said as if she hadn't been listening to a word either of them had said. 'You know very well I can't read. Come with me to the kitchen, Liza. Wendy, run upstairs to Letitia and tell Nanny George I sent you.'

Wendy's face went grey and she felt cold and dizzy. 'Is she –'

Nellie let out a sigh and put her hands on Wendy's shoulders. 'Letitia is in bed. The last I heard of her, she was having her breakfast brought up on a tray.'

Wendy stared. 'You mean, she isn't dead?'

'Dead? Certainly not.' Nellie pulled a face. 'I can tell you, things would be a lot more peaceful in this house if she was.'

Letitia dipped a toast finger into her soft-boiled egg. 'You're not cross with me, Wendy, are you?' She nibbled delicately and wiped her mouth with a napkin. 'You see, I said to myself, Letitia, how can you be so unkind? Imagine how sad everyone would be. And the expense . . . Everyone dressed in black for months, maybe years. I mean, I know I was angry with Mama.' She dipped in another finger of toast. 'I'm still not speaking to her yet, by the way.'

Wendy sat on the edge of Letitia's bed. When she first saw her sitting there in her pink frilly bedjacket with the satin bows down the front, she had wanted to grab the breakfast tray and tip it over her head. Then she noticed that the round-faced, furious Letitia of yesterday wasn't there any more. In her place was someone who seemed to have shrunk. And even though the cunning hadn't gone from her eyes, the fight had gone from her body.

'It's like playing whist,' explained Letitia. She wiped her mouth again. 'Do you play cards?'

'No.'

'But you know what a trump card means, don't you?'

'Of course I do, you feathered-headed moron.'

Letitia sighed and lay back on her pillows. 'I probably deserve that unkind cut.'

'You were talking about cards.'

'Yes.' Letitia sat up. 'You see, it occurred to me that my death – or, more accurately, my *threat* of death – is my trump card.' She pushed away her breakfast tray. 'And good cards don't come up often, so I would be foolish not to hold on to this one for as long as I can.' Letitia fixed Wendy with her glittering monkey eyes. 'Mama told me that once. About good cards, I mean.'

Wendy stood up and handed Letitia back her letter. 'Just in case you need it for another time. All you have to do is cross out my name.'

'You're not angry with me, are you?' asked Letitia again.

Wendy patted Letitia's hand and walked out of the room.

Wendy

* * *

Wendy sat beside Esther and looked out at the ducks on the pond. 'I'm glad Letitia isn't dead,' she said.

Esther smiled ruefully. 'Letitia threatens to kill herself almost every time she doesn't get what she wants. I'm sorry you were dragged into it.'

'I don't mind,' said Wendy. Letitia had done her the biggest favour of her life. Without her, she would never have found out about Thomas. Now, somehow, she wanted to repay the favour. 'Poor Letitia. The thing is, Esther, she hates the idea of moving to Saundersbane so much.' She tried to choose the right words. 'But really, I think she's frightened.'

Esther frowned. 'Letitia is such a selfish little baggage and you're such a good friend to her. To tell you the truth, I can't really understand why.'

'I don't know either. Most of the time I'd rather play with an orang-utan.' Wendy remembered the favour.

'But it's horrible when someone is so unhappy.'

'Letitia will always be unhappy because she thinks she's hard done by.' Esther let out a breath and watched it turn to steam. 'Part of it's my fault.'

'But you've never done anything to Letitia,' said Wendy. 'It was her always trying to get you into trouble.'

'She was paying me back.'

Wendy looked at Esther in astonishment. 'What for?'

'I'm almost twenty-one. Letitia is ten. She needs her father more than I do and I've never let him go. For a long time, it was just the two of us. And my mother was very different from Lady Cunningham.' Esther shook her head. 'I could never understand why he married her. She's everything my mother wasn't – showy, exotic, even exciting, I suppose. Anyway, I used to blame her for making him unhappy. Now I understand that he is as much to blame as she is. Every day, he compares her to my mother and I encourage it. Not that either of us says anything, but I can see it in his face. He hates her for what she is. But that's what she was like when he married her. I remember, you see.' Esther smiled sadly. 'Of course, she tried to disguise it. She pretended to be interested in butterflies, like he was, but she didn't fool anyone. She couldn't stand the smell of the killing bottles, poor woman.' Esher rubbed her gloved hand over her face. 'Goodness me, I didn't mean to make a speech.'

Wendy said nothing. It was so easy to understand things when Esther explained them. But there was only one question that mattered to her. 'Do you think your father loves Letitia and Henry and Lady Cunningham?'

Esther took a deep breath. 'I think he does. But I think they can only be a proper family if they are on their own, without me.'

'So you won't be going with them to Northumberland?'

Esther shook her head. 'I love Saundersbane, but it's time I got on with my own life. I shall buy myself a little house with Nellie to look after me and devote my time to my work with the movement.' She smiled. 'Not many suffragettes have their own money at twenty-one. I want to do something useful with mine.'

Wendy laughed. 'Letitia always said that rich people have a responsibility to do useful things. That usually meant me asking for new toys for her to play with.' She shrugged. 'Anyway, now it's all different.'

'What do you mean?'

'Father's broke. I heard him tell Mother.'

'You mustn't worry about things you don't understand,' cried Esther, dismayed. 'The police have dropped their charges against him, so he's bound to find another job soon.' She took Wendy's hand. 'Poor thing. That's why I wanted to talk to you today. You seemed so strange the last time. All that talk about Colney Hatch.'

'It was that poor mad boy,' said Wendy.

'You mean Alice's brother?'

There was a silence.

Wendy stared out over the grey water of the Round Pond. So many terrible things had happened. Not only to herself but to Mother and, as she now knew, to Father as well. Because the more that Wendy thought about it, the more she was sure that it was Lady Cunningham who had decided to capture Father, and he was too flattered to tell her to shut up. All she had to do was ask him to take her driving in his motor car. Wendy shook her head. He was such a show-off.

Such a lovely show-off when he was happy.

'Why are you shaking your head?'

'I was thinking about motor cars,' said Wendy. 'I hate them.'

Esther laughed. 'So do I. But I'm afraid that makes us very old-fashioned.'

Wendy thought about Rosegrove and the dusty country lanes rutted with cart tracks and marked with horses' hooves. She remembered the smell of wild honeysuckle in the hedges. And she thought about Thomas. By sending Thomas to live in the country, her mother had done the best she could for him. And as for Father, he must have loved Thomas too. Why else would he have comforted Mother last night? She sighed. Everything to do with grown-ups was so complicated.

'Wendy, are you *sure* there's nothing you want to tell me?'

Wendy looked into Esther's clear green eyes. She knew they would never talk like this again, because soon Esther would be a proper grown-up. If Wendy told her about Thomas, her secret would be destroyed.

'Wendy, please. If you're unhappy –'

'I'm not unhappy. Actually, I'm happier now than I've ever been before.' She wanted to say something that would give Esther some kind of answer. It was what you had to do with grown-ups, then they left you alone. Wendy smiled and took Esther's hand. 'I get this strange feeling in my head and I don't know what's real and what's made up.'

Esther laughed and kissed her forehead. 'Everyone feels like that sometimes.'

But Wendy knew exactly why she got that strange feeling. It came from listening to grown-ups too much. She picked up a flat stone and flicked it onto the pond. It bounced five times, which was one more than her record.

As soon as Wendy walked through the door into the front hall, she could feel the house was completely different. It was as if everything in it had been taken down, washed, hung out to dry and put back again.

'Father's cut his moustache off,' cried John as Wendy came into the nursery. 'And he's got a new job.

Mother says it's much more fun than the last one.'

Michael climbed onto a chair. 'And he's sold his car!' he shouted.

Liza laughed. 'For goodness' *sake,* boys!'

'What did Esther say?' asked John.

Wendy shrugged. 'Nothing much. She's going to stay in London with Nellie and buy a little house. How's Letitia?'

'Just after you left, she went out with Lady Cunningham to buy a fur-lined cape.' John snorted. 'Do you know what she said to me?'

'What?'

'Only really smart people live in the country.'

Wendy burst out laughing.

'Gracious!' cried Liza. 'With all the noise, I almost forgot.' She picked up a flat brown-paper package from the nursery dresser and handed it to Wendy. 'It's from your Uncle Arthur.'

'Open it up!' shouted Michael.

'What's inside it?' cried John.

But Liza was watching Wendy's face and she knew she wanted to be left alone. 'Come along with me,' said Liza briskly to Michael and John. 'There's two pairs of shoes to be polished if you're going to go to the pantomime tomorrow.'

Wendy sat down on the faded chintz armchair by the window and looked at her name written in Uncle Arthur's beautiful italic handwriting. Slowly and carefully, she untied the string and unwrapped the brown paper. A sheet of thick cream vellum floated onto the floor.

My dear Wendy,

How quiet Rosegrove seems without you all here! Your Aunt Emily and I rattle about in the house like two peas in a drum. I am writing with news of Thomas.

* * *

Here Wendy's heart banged in her chest. She clenched the paper in both hands and forced herself to keep reading.

I know you have always been fond of Thomas and that you visit him every time you come to Rosegrove. Last month a friend of mine who is a painter came to stay. I told him about Thomas and his drawings and he asked to see them. He was astounded by how good they were – particularly the ones Thomas had drawn from an aerial perspective. Mrs Crocker told me you had been reading to Thomas about aeroplanes. The upshot of this is to tell you that my friend would like to exhibit a collection of Thomas's drawings at some point in the future and that Mrs Crocker has asked me to tell you specially that Thomas is happier now than he has ever been before. None of us know why. We can only guess that it has something to do with the joy he has discovered in the idea of things flying. And that, my dear Wendy, is all because of you. I enclose a drawing he wanted you to have. Our best love to you all and I hope we will see you at Christmas. Your loving Uncle Arthur

Wendy lifted out a piece of card wrapped in tissue paper. Inside was a picture of a bird flying over an emerald ocean. Its white wings were tipped with turquoise and a tuft of silver feathers circled its head like a crown. But it wasn't the movement and the beauty of the soaring wings that Wendy stared at. It was the bird's face under the crown of feathers. It was her face and, for the first time for as long as she could remember, she looked strong and free and full of joy. At that moment, Wendy knew as surely as if Thomas was in the room with her that he felt the same way too.

She put the picture away in her drawer. One day she would show it to John and Michael, but not now. She wanted to keep it her secret for a little while longer.

John and Michael were asleep when Wendy pulled on her dressing gown and opened the nursery door. She was sure it would be empty as usual, but she was wrong. Liza was sitting by the coal fire, trimming her Christmas hat with an ostrich feather that Mrs Darling had given her. Wendy looked over to Nana's basket. It was empty.

'Can't you sleep?'

'Where's Nana?'

'Please don't fuss about Nana,' said Liza wearily. 'She's outside tonight because, with all the comings and goings, I haven't even had time to clean the nursery and the place is covered in dog's hair.'

'It's not that.' Wendy held out an envelope. 'I want to give Mother a letter.'

Liza sighed. 'Is it about all those things you heard? Because they aren't true and you mustn't think about them ever again.'

Wendy smiled. It was the easiest thing to do. 'I've forgotten all about them already.'

'Good girl,' said Liza, smiling back. 'Now, are you sure your letter can't wait till tomorrow?'

'I'm sure.'

Liza looked into Wendy's face. Everything about it seemed to have changed, but the whys and hows were none of her business. 'Off you go, then, but be quick.'

Wendy tiptoed down the stairs. There was a light under the door and, for a moment, she was afraid that her mother was still in her room. Then she heard her parents' voices below, so she pulled open the bedroom door and stepped quickly inside.

Wendy stared in amazement around her. The floor was covered in evening clothes. It was as if Mother had tried on all of her dresses – which was odd, because they were dining on their own that night. A door slammed somewhere in the house and made Wendy jump. She walked quickly over to the dressing table and pulled open the middle drawer. Then she put back all the money she had stolen, except for the sixpence she had spent on sweets for John and Michael, and a short letter telling her mother she had taken it in the first place. Whatever happened now, Wendy didn't want anyone to be blamed for something she had done, and somehow she didn't think her mother would be angry. She was about to walk out of the room when she saw her mother's pearl satin robe edged with swan's-down. She picked it up and squeezed it in her arms. It smelled delicious.

Wendy stepped onto the landing as her mother and father walked into the hallway. Her mother wore a white gown that fell from her shoulders and trailed along the floor. She looked like the angel in Thomas's drawing. Wendy watched as her father took her mother's hand almost shyly in his. Without his moustache, he looked much younger. 'I love you,' he said. He kissed her on the forehead. 'I'll always love you.'

Wendy stood on the stairs. She didn't care if they saw her. She was never going to crouch behind the banisters again.

Wendy

* * *

That night, snow fell for the first time. Wendy stood by the window. There was a full moon in the sky and the ground sparkled as if it was covered in tiny diamonds. It was a new white world that seemed frozen in time. Wendy climbed into bed and fell into a deep sleep. She dreamed she was flying and that Thomas was flying to meet her. But it wasn't the Thomas with the wide shoulders and long square-jawed face. It was the boy who lived in Thomas's mind, a young Thomas who would never grow up, a boy whom Wendy loved with all of her heart.

They circled around each other high above the emerald ocean. Then they flew to a place that glittered with the colours of a thousand rainbows that grown-ups will never be able to see.

About the Author

Karen Wallace is the author of more than eighty books for children. Her first novel, *Raspberries on the Yangtze,* was short-listed for the Guardian Children's Fiction Award in England, while *Climbing the Monkey Puzzle Tree,* was a *Sunday Times* Book of the Week there. *Wendy* is her second novel to be published in the United States.

Karen was born in Canada and spent her childhood running wild by the banks of Quebec's Gatineau River. At the age of eleven she was sent to boarding school in England. She now lives in Herefordshire with her husband, novelist Sam Llewellyn, her sons, and two large cats called Cougar and Dave.